The Best Brownie Recipe

Recipe
A Short Story collection

B. Heather Mantler

Table of Contents

This volume is a accumulation of years of work and because of that many people have helped me with each story. My family being the most likely to be asked to provide feedback. The members of the Prince George writing group have also helped me with many of these pieces. So, thank you to everyone who gave me their suggestions on how to improve these pieces.

JUST TALKING

"So, which of us goes first?" Patrick asked looking for the game board, "I haven't played in so long, I can't remember."

"The black side starts," Robert sat down in his chair and got comfortable.

"That means me, I guess," Patrick said as he studied the placement of the pieces. He moved one near the middle to the black space diagonal from the black space it was sitting on. "How was the conference?"

"Same as last year," Robert answered, "Nothing new to report, but there may be some changes next year due to the lower attendance."

"I'll wait and see about that," Patrick said.

"How has your day been?" Robert asked as he did the same to his red piece on the left side of the board.

"I think I have to kill David," Patrick kept his eyes on the board as he moved his piece another square.

"But why?" Robert looked up from the board at his friend, "He had been your money maker for so long."

"He is getting tiring, doing the same old stuff day in and day out," Patrick watched Robert moved his piece before jumping over it. He picked up the shot glass and pouring the gin down his throat. Patrick shook his head clear before putting the piece to the side.

"That is the reason why everyone loves him," Robert moved another piece forward, "He is everyone's perfect man."

"He is too perfect," Patrick studied the board for a minute before shifting a different piece.

"Too perfect?" Robert took his turn, but was not close enough to jump Patrick's piece.

"His smile always melts the heart of whichever woman is in front of him," Patrick moved his piece another square away from Robert's piece, "They all swoon in his presence, while the men stand up straighter and call him champ. The man wouldn't fall on his backside if I gave him banana peels for slippers and greased the floor with w-40. In fact, he would use the lubrication to catch some woman who fainted due to the glint of the sun off his teeth."

"So, give him a flaw," Robert said, "Something he can't turn around on him."

"Like what?" Patrick asked.

"Make him an alcoholic," Robert jumped Patrick's piece and tossed back the shot glass of gin before putting the piece beside the board.

"Won't work," Patrick moved his piece into the corner Robert had freed up. He placed a olive on a toothpick from the bowl into the shot glass.

"Why not?" Robert considered the board for a moment before changed squares of his piece, "He gets drunk, falls off a bar stool, and ends up thrown out of the bar."

"At which point he wanders into an alley where he stumbles on a woman being attacked," Patrick moved another piece forward, "She of course falls for him because he saved her and she takes him back to her place, where he spends the night on the couch and wakes up hangover free. It doesn't work because he is David. I could get him hooked on meth and somehow he would use it to come out on top."

"That is a problem. What are you going to do about it?"

"I think I'm going to kill him off," Patrick jumped two of Robert's pieces and tosses one back after the other, "In some way that means he can never come back to haunt me again."

"What about all of his fans?" Robert jumped Patrick's piece and swallowed the gin before putting the piece to one side.

"I have to make his end fitting enough for them to accept it. I'm still working on that part. What is the best way to murder someone?"

"Fall from a cliff, shot in the back, drowned in the bathtub, run over by a car, blown up while defusing a bomb, attacked by a wild animal, tossed through a wood chipper, suffocated with a plastic bag, knifed in the street by a thug," Robert gulped down the gin from the piece he jumped, "Poisoning, bludgeoned by a candlestick, neck snapped, crushed by a gargoyle, clubbed in the head with a tire iron, dissolved in battery acid, asphyxiated with carbon monoxide, weighed down by cement overshoes, strangled with piano wire, squeezed between shipping containers, hung from the rafters, a thousand cuts with a razor blade, tied to the front of a cannon."

"That is a lot of options," Patrick dropped another olive in the shot glass, which had reached the corner.

"I've time to think about it," Robert jumped another of Patrick's pieces and drank the gin.

"Of course."

"So, what sounds best for David? Or which do you think David can't get out of?"

"Still working that out," Patrick watched as Robert ate the olive out of the glass his piece had jumped before drinking the gin from the glass.

The men did not speak for several minutes as they

played the game. Patrick was taking out more of Robert's pieces, but the alcohol did not seem to be affecting his judgement too much. Each man focused on the pieces moving around the board rather than the other. Some turns went fast and others took a minute. The number of pieces slowly went down, until Robert had only two and Patrick had four.

"Have you thought about what you are going to do when David is gone?" Robert interrupted the quiet.

"Maybe I'll tell the story of the wood chipper operator," Patrick jumped Robert's second to last piece and downed the gin. Robert examined the board for any place for his last piece to go.

"Cornered," Robert sighed before picking up his last shot glass and held it out. Patrick picked up one of his own leftover glasses. "To the death of David, the perfect man, and the resurrection of your muse."

The glasses clinked and the men downed their gin.

The Best Brownie Recipe

NOTES

A Moral story was originally written as a speech. I have given it as a speech twice and have received good response. The Toastmasters manual is the Storytelling manual and this project is telling a moral story. According to the manual, evaluator is supposed to decide whether the twist at the end was good or not.

A MORAL STORY

Two foxes were sunning themselves beside a river. It was a beautiful day and they were enjoying it. The squirrel came up to them. Now the squirrel is the messenger of the forest because he is quick on his feet and speaks fast. He isn't always understood when he is in a hurry, but otherwise he is a good messenger.

"There is a guy named Aesop sitting in a clearing in the forest," the squirrel chattered, "He is looking for animals to be stars in his stories. If you want to be part of a story you need to got to the clearing and talk to him."

The one fox jumped up.

"That sounds great," the fox said. The second fox didn't move.

"Don't you want to star in one of Aesop's stories?" the first fox asked.

"No, I think I will stay here and enjoy this beautiful day," the second fox replied.

So the first fox went off. He was laughing to himself at his friend's foolishness. Oh well, he would be famous and his friend would be jealous.

The fox found a grey haired man sitting on a tree stump

with parchment and a quill. The man was scribbling something on the parchment. The fox cleared his throat to call attention to himself without appearing to disturb the man. The man glanced up at him before looking back at the parchment. He continued to scribble for a few more minutes. Finally he put the quill in the bottle of ink that was sitting on the grass. The man raised his head to look at the fox.

"Are you Aesop?" the fox asked.

"I am," the man answered.

"I was told that you are looking for animals to be part of your stories," the fox said.

"I am," the man said, "Would you like to be part of the Fox and the Goat?"

"Certainly," the fox answered. He wasn't worried about sharing the spotlight with the goat because everyone knew that a fox was superior to a goat.

A goat came into the clearing from the other side. It looked like he had been waiting.

"I'll tell the story," Aesop said, "One day a goat was wandering lost in the woods."

The goat took on a lost look and began meandering around the clearing.

"Now a fox happened along and saw the goat. The fox decided that the goat looked like a very good lunch. But attacking the goat straight on could get him knocked into a local geographic feature. So the fox was going to have to use his intelligence if he wanted goat for lunch.

The fox went over to the goat and asked, 'what is wrong?'

'I can't find my family,' the goat replied, 'I turned around and they had moved and now I can't find them.'

'I know these woods quite well,' the fox said, 'I can help you find your family.'

'I don't know where to start looking,' the goat said.

'We can start by going up to the hill nearby and look

around,' the fox said." The fox and the goat headed for the hill with Aesop following behind them.

"As they were going up the hill the fox was following the goat and looking for his chance to attack the goat's hind legs. The fox was so intend on the goat that he missed seeing the hole in the ground. His foot went in and caused him to lose his balance and tumble down the hill."

The fox found himself hitting every rock on his way down the hill until he finally crashed into a briar bush. As he got up and dusted himself off the Fox wasn't sure he liked the kind of story he had gotten himself into. But he trotted back up the hill to where the goat and Aesop were waiting.

"'I can see my family from here,' the goat said. The fox looked out and saw a group of white spots in a field just beyond the river.

'I know where that is,' the fox said, 'I'll show you a place where you can cross the river." So the fox led the way down the hill with the goat and Aesop following.

Once at the river the fox led the way to a log that stretched across it. The goat climbed up on the log, but before he could get to the top the fox tried biting at his hind legs. The goat kicked out just in time to hit the fox before the fox to get to him. The fox fell into the river with a splash and was quickly carried away by the current.

From his resting place the second fox heard the cries of the first fox as he went passed. The second fox smiled to himself. He knew that is was not a good idea to be a fox in an Aesop fable.

B. Heather Mantler

GINGERBREAD ARMY

She was the sweetest old lady on the street. The kids around could always ring her doorbell and be greeted by a tray of cookies for them to pick from. The parents didn't mind her as she had a nice smile and a warm greeting for everyone she met. But the grumpy old man across the street just growled in her direction whenever he saw her and his caretakers would have to take him back inside.

It was the middle of December now and Miss Connors had been going out to the store every day. She always came home with grocery store bags full of flour, sugar, molasses, and gumdrops. Mr. Hardly across the street sat at his front window with binoculars and trying to see what she was doing with all that stuff. The rest of the block put up lights, played in the snow, and went about the stress of holiday cheer. This had been going on since the first day of December and with it being the middle of the month Miss Connors's house smelled of gingerbread to anyone going by on the street.

The children from the street would knock on Miss Connors's door, but she merely smiled and offered them sugar cookies. Despite the drool-worthy smell, the children accepted the sugar cookies before going away. Many others would stop to smell the air and then move on with smiles on their faces.

Mr. Hardly stayed by the window and studied the situation. Despite his caregivers trying to get him to move and do other things, he kept his vigil. He knew that Miss Connors was up to something and he was going to find out what it was. But all she seemed to be doing was baking and bringing home more ingredients.

The days slid by, but Mr. Hardly spent his time watching out the window. He barely noticed when his caretakers put up the Christmas tree, decorated the house, and discreetly placed wrapped packages beneath the tree. If he was not so focused on his surveillance, he might have even had flights of fancy where he shopped for gifts to give in return. Unfortunately, he was not able to go out by himself to do such shopping. All his shopping was done by his caretakers.

Christmas Eve was a quiet day as the adults were getting ready and the children were inside impatiently waiting for Santa to arrive. There was no new snow, so the children had little else to do but wait. Miss Connors was not seen at all, but the smell of gingerbread floated around her house almost to the point of being able to see it. Mr. Hardly continued his surveillance, despite attempts from his caretakers to tempt him away from the window. Not even discussion of his favourite meal was enough to tempt him away.

Night fell and the lights around the neighbourhood went out. Some left the strings of Christmas lights glowing, but most turned them off. Mr. Hardly sat by the window while his caretakers turned off the lights around him. The only house where the lights stayed on was Miss Connors' house. Not the ones in the front rooms, but one further back in the house. Mr. Hardly watched Miss Connors' house and waited. He was sure that this was the night things were going to happen.

It got later and later. Mr. Hardly was tired from many days of surveillance and he found his eyes drooping. He blinked to try and stay awake. Mr. Hardly felt his chin reach his chest and jerked it back up. He shook it in hopes it would clear the tiredness. If he could, Mr. Hardly would have made himself a pot of coffee, but that was beyond what he was able to do and his caretaker had gone to bed.

His eyes started to close again, but this time when he blinked them open briefly Mr. Hardly saw movement at Miss Connors' house. This woke him completely as he watched Santa's sleigh land on the roof. Before he could step out, Santa was swarmed by gingerbreadmen cookies. Santa was quickly tied up and dragged down from the roof. The gingerbread cookies took Santa inside.

Mr. Hardly reached back to try to unlocked his wheelchair, but he could not find the lever. The gingerbread cookies climbed into the sleigh while others exchanged the bag of toys in the back for boxes. Then Miss Connors climbed out the highest window in her house and then carefully got up to the sleigh. She climbed in and got herself comfortable. She was wearing a parka and the gingerbread cookies had brought her a blanket.

Without any way to get his wheelchair working, Mr. Hardly undid the strap from around his waist that held him in. He collapsed forward and caught himself on the window sill. Mr. Hardly lowered his weakened limbs to the floor and then pulled himself across to the table where the phone sat. He grabbed the phone and started to dial the number he knew from heart. He put the phone to his ear.

"Hello?" the male voice had a high squeak to it.

"It is Agent H," Mr. Hardly said, "And this is an emergency."

"You are retired," the male voice answered.

"I know," Mr. Hardly said, "But this is an emergency."

"The fat man is busy," the male voice said.

"No," Mr. Hardly replied, "He has just been kidnapped by Miss Cookie and she is now spreading her army as far across the world as she can. My last mission was to keep surveillance on Miss Cookie."

"Are you sure about this, Agent H?" the male voice squeaked at a much higher pitched.

"I just saw her get into the sleigh," Mr. Hardly said.

He looked out the window and saw the sleigh rise off the roof with Miss Connors at the reins. Cookies were keeping her company.

"She is getting away," Mr. Hardly said.

"We are tracking the sleigh," the male voice squeaked, "It appears to be on track."

"There is nothing I can do from here," Mr. Hardly said, "You need to send someone to help the fat man."

"We are tracking the sleigh," the squeaky voice said, "We will send out teams as soon as we can." The line went dead. Mr. Hardly set the phone back in the stand and picked it up again, but there was no dial tone. Fear gripped Mr. Hardly as he sat on the floor of his living room in the dark. He quietly put the phone back and listened for any sounds of intruders.

The lights on the tree, which his caretakers had left on, went out as did any other light in the house. Mr. Hardly could not hear anything movement from inside, but he doubted that would last long. He had to do something. Mr. Hardly rolled himself on to his stomach and dragged himself across the floor using his arms.

He headed into the kitchen. It was a long trip along the floor. He stopped on the threshold between the kitchen and the living room. There was some noise at the front door. It sounded like rodents of some kind. Mr. Hardly tried to hurry in his journey into the kitchen. He pulled himself over the threshold and looked around the dark kitchen for some sort of a weapon. There were knives in the knife block, but Mr. Hardly doubted they would do much against cookies. The noises at the front door was louder as whatever was out there was trying to get in.

Mr. Hardly sat up and opened the fridge. He took out the four litre jug of milk his caretaker had bought earlier in the day. Mr. Hardly closed the fridge door and moved to the middle of the clear area of the kitchen. He sloshed the milk in a circle around him making sure there was plenty of milk and no spaces the cookies could get through. He also had some milk still in the jug, which he set down on the floor in front of him. Now there was nothing to do but wait.

The noise at the front door got louder and then there was the sound of the door opening. Then it sounded like rodents skittering across the floor. In the light coming in the kitchen window, Mr. Hardly could see the gingerbread cookies coming towards him. There were more than a dozen of them. Their first few steps in the milk didn't affect them at all, but then the milk started soaking into the cookie making them soggy.

The soggy feet caused the cookies to collapse into the milk. At first they tried to shake it off and continue moving forward, but the more the milk absorbed into the cookie the harder it was for them to move. The first dozen or so cookies succumb to the milk, but the next cookies used the bodies of their comrades to get closer to Mr. Hardly. The ones that came next just lied down in the milk to help the cookies behind them to cross.

Mr. Hardly splashed milk toward the cookies. This hit them and caused them to be pushed backwards. The cookies paused as if they were taking stock of the situation. Then they started coming again. Mr. Hardly waited until they had reached the last of fallen cookies before tossing more milk at them. This slowed them down again.

This fight continued in this way. The cookies made little progress beyond what they had already and Mr. Hardly was slowly running out of milk. There did not seem to be any end of cookies. Mr. Hardly, however, knew that both his ammunition and energy was very limited. Both were getting low.

There was more noise coming from the front door. This time it was much bigger than cookies. In fact there was the sound of cookies being broken. Some of the cookies stopped moving towards Mr. Hardly and instead went back towards the door. However, plenty of them still came towards Mr. Hardly. In less than a minute a figured stood in the doorway to the kitchen. It appeared to be male, about three feet in height and some extra weight around the middle. Both his hat and shoes had a curl at the end. The man was swinging a cane in his hand, which was what was breaking the cookies. .

"Agent H?" the man asked.

"I am unharmed," Mr. Hardly replied.

The man waved his hand and the electricity came back on as the kitchen lights also came on. The cookies were either soggy or broken into pieces. It didn't matter which they had stopped moving.

"What about the fat man?" Mr. Hardly asked.

"He has his own rescue team," the man answered.

"Miss. Cookie?" Mr. Hardly asked.

"Still working on it," the man answered, "We have been tracking the location of the sleigh. We have not been able to get an intercept team close enough to actually contact the sleigh or capture its occupants. But we are working on it."

There was more noise at the front door. This time Santa and his rescue team stepped into the doorway. Santa looked over the mess on the floor in front of Mr. Hardly.

"Despite your retirement, you have not lost your edge," Santa said with a nod of approval.

"We need to get Miss. Cookie," Mr. Hardly said.

"Yes," Santa said, "But there is nothing we can do from here. I am told there is a team on the way. You have done plenty at the risk of your own safety. Don't worry about the rest; I paused time when I was grabbed and I have not started it again. No one will notice anything happened."

There was a beep from the man's pocket. He took out his phone and started pushing buttons.

"The intercept team is thirty seconds behind the sleigh and closing," the man reported, "Shouldn't be long now."

"Help Agent H clean this mess," Santa instructed his rescue team.

Mr. Hardly stayed where he was as he watched the team clean up the cookies and milk. They removed the milk jug and placed a new one in the fridge. Once the kitchen floor was clean enough they brought Mr. Hardly's wheelchair in. They helped Mr. Hardly into his chair. He wheeled himself to the front room window and put on the brake. Mr. Hardly could still hear some activity in the kitchen. Santa sat down in the chair beside Mr. Hardly.

"Thank you for the help," Santa said.

"That was why I was placed here," Mr. Hardly said.

"But even with that," Santa said, "I thank you. Is there anything I can do in return?"

"I wish I was able to get gifts for my caretakers," Mr. Hardly said.

"What would you like to give them?" Santa asked.

Mr. Hardly listed the items and which was for who.

"Granted," Santa said. He nodded towards the tree and gift wrapped packages were appeared there.

The rescue teams came into the living room.

"Everything is ready," the man reported, "And we have caught Miss. Cookie."

"Good," Santa said getting to his feet.

Mr. Hardly saw the sleigh land on Miss. Cookie's roof. Miss. Cookie was not in it, instead there were two elves driving it. Mr. Hardly heard the front door close and lock. Santa and his team walked across to the yards and climb back up into his sleigh.

Mr. Hardly blinked and the sleigh was gone. Time must have started again. There was the sound of someone moving in the bedrooms. A moment later, Mr. Hardly turned to see his overnight caretaker come into the living room.

"Are you still up?" she asked, "Let's get you to bed." She came over and unlocked the brake. Mr. Hardly felt the exhaustion of the last month and was more than willing to let himself be put to bed. He checked over his shoulder one more time to make sure the presents were there. They were. He smiled.

The Best Brownie Recipe

NOTES

The idea for Airplane Gone came while I was visiting my grandparents during the spring of 2014. They would listen to the news every evening as they ate supper. During this period the major story was an airplane that had gone missing. I do not remember exactly what happened to the plane; I think they may be fishing the pieces out of the ocean still. But it was not as fun or entertaining as the idea I had.

AIRPLANE GONE

This article appeared on the front page of the Western Central Chronicle on March 11.

Airplane Missing!

Air central flight 741 disappeared on its way from North America to Europe. There were 235 people on board. The flight took off on time from the Central International Airport and disappeared from radar before it had left the continent. The area where the last transmission came from was searched, but no trace has been found. The transport authorities and law enforcement agencies are on the lookout for any sign of what happened. A press conference with updated information is set for tomorrow morning.

At this point they do not know if it was a mechanical problem or a terrorist plot, or some other scenario. The authorities are currently going through the passenger list to see if anyone suspicious boarded the plane. They are interviewing all the airline staff to see if security protocol was followed and whether there needs to be any changes to security procedures.

This article appeared on the front page of the Western

Central Chronicle on March 12.

Person of Interest in the Disappearance of Flight 741

Yesterday flight 741 went missing mid-air and the wreckage has not been found. At this morning's press conference, it was announced that there is a person of interest in the disappearance of the plane. Law enforcement agencies are currently looking for a man they say was carrying a fake passport when he boarded the flight. He is described as a Caucasian male, about five foot eight inches, a hundred and seventy pounds, with brown hair, and blue eyes. It is believed the man is between forty and fifty years of age. The passport was in the name Jonathan Current. If you recognize him or have any information about this man, you are asked to contact...

No more information on the location of the plane is available as the investigation is ongoing and nothing from the plane has been located. According to the airline's CEO, all security measures were followed exactly as they should be and no one on that flight was considered a security risk. Even the man the police are looking for, Jonathan Current, did not trigger any alarms. The airline is putting out a list of the missing passenger over the next few days.

This article appeared on the front page of the Western Central Chronicle on March 13.

No News on Missing Plane

Seventy-two hours after the disappearance of flight 741, authorities are no closer to solving the mystery of what happened to it. No wreckage had turned up. Nothing has been heard from any of the 235 passengers. The recording from the co-pit gives no indication that the plane was in any danger. In fact everything seemed to be normal up until the plane disappeared.

The authorities are still trying to identify who the false Jonathan Current is and has found that there is no other information about the man. No one has come forward with any knowledge as to who he is and the authorities have not traced him back to a real identity.

The airline has also released the list of passenger and reported that they have contacted the families to let them know that their relatives are missing. The airline is also asking the families to stay home and wait the airline to give them any news. The CEO has promised that as soon as the airline knows anything they will get the word out to the families.

This article appeared on the third page of the Western Central Chronicle on March 15.

Fake Passport was Stolen

The person of interest in the disappearance of Flight 741 did not have a fake passport as first announced, but it was in fact stolen. The owner of the passport is a resident of the city. Jonathan Current reported the robbery to the police after he figured out the passport was missing, which was after reading the article in the paper with the name of the man who was the person of interest. It is unknown the exact date of the robbery and the police say that nothing else appears to have been stolen.

The police are asking the people along the street Mr. Current lives on whether they had seen anything strange over the past few weeks. Mr. Current himself has been on a business trip until the day before flight 741 went missing.

The transportation authorities have been giving daily updates on the information they have about the flight and their investigation into where it went, however little information has been added to what is already known. They have the last radar position of the plane without any sign of wreckage. Security at other airports have been stepped up in recent days, but they have not cancelled any flights.

This article appeared on the third page of the Western Central Chronicle on March 29.

First Passenger From Flight 741 Found

Yesterday afternoon Penny Rose arrived home by taxi after she took flight 741 to visit family in Europe. Flight 741 disappeared mid-flight and no trace of it has been found by the authorities. The police have questioned Mrs. Rose and found that she has no memory of what happened. She remembered getting on the plane and falling asleep. The next thing she remembered was in the taxi heading home. Mrs. Rose claims she does not know anything about what has happened over the last few weeks, or what happened to the plane.

Mrs. Rose's relatives in Europe reported that she never arrived for the expected visit and they hope she can come visit another time. The airline's spokesman would not comment as to whether they would they would reimburse Mrs. Rose for the flight or provide her with a complimentary flight to make up for the visit she did not get with her relatives.

The transport authorities still have no information about what happened to the plane or where the rest of the passengers are. The police, however, have been in contact with the relatives of all the other passengers in case others reappear. They are asking for any information that anyone can provide.

This article appeared on the sixth page of the Western Central Chronicle on April 4.

Passengers From Flight 741 Home Safe

Passengers from flight 741 have been returning to their homes safely over the last week. It started when Penny Rose returned to her home in a taxi with no memory of what happened. A few days later Ian and Beth Leitch returned to their home in Europe by taxi. They had been on a rock climbing trip and were headed home on flight 741. According to the police, the couple has no memories of anything after getting on the flight and falling asleep. The next thing they remembered was being in the taxi, which dropped them off at home. The taxi driver said that he had picked them up at the airport and took them to the address they gave him.

Authorities have gone over the security video from the airport, but have no footage of the Leitchs before they were at the taxi stand waiting for a ride. The authorities have also reported that several others from the flight have also returned home, both here in North America and in Europe, with no memory of what happened to the plane. In total fifty passengers have been reported safe. No trace of the plane has turned up and the authorities are still investigating the whole incident.

This article appeared on the sixth page of the Western Central Chronicle on April 19.

All Passengers From Flight 741 Accounted For

All the passengers from Flight 741, which disappeared without a trace back in March, have all been found safe and accounted for. Each were found in taxi line up at airport or in the taxis on their way home. None of the passengers remember what happened on the plane, or anything before being found. They claimed to fall asleep on the plane and woke up on their way home. The airline staff have also turned up at their homes, however, they were not connected to taxi. Instead they merely appeared on their own doorsteps with no memory of what happened. The stewardesses fell asleep about the time the rest of the passenger did. The pilots remembered everything up until the plane fell off the radar.

There has been no sign of the plane itself and authorities have no clues as to what happened to it. They are still investigating and are asking that if anyone knows something that they contact the proper authorities.

The person of interest, the fake Jonathan Current, remains the only person on board the plane who they have not found. They are no closer to finding out who the man is than they did back in the March when they announced him as a person of interest.

This article appeared on the eighth page of the Western Central Chronicle on April 28.

Airplane Found!

The mystery of flight 741 is far from solved, but the plane has been found. It turned up in the repair bay owned by the airline. In was in a back corner and the airline has no idea how long it was sitting there before it was noticed by one of their mechanics.

Flight 741 disappeared while on its way to Europe back in March and the authorities have been investigating the incident ever since. So far, all the passengers have been found returning to their homes with no memory of what happened. The staff returned in the same manner. The only person of interest has not turned up and the authorities have found no way of identifying the man, who used a stolen passport to board the plane.

The authorities are continuing ask the public that they pass on any information they may know. Also if anyone saw anything usual that day. They are also wondering if any of the passenger, crew, airline staff, or other travellers might have spoken to the false Jonathan Current during the time before the plane boarded. If you count among that group the authorities are asking to talk to you.

This advertisement appeared in the classified section of the Western Central Chronicle on April 30.

Turn Over

Well, Mr. Smith, I made the plane disappear. Your turn.

The Best Brownie Recipe

B. Heather Mantler

I LOVED HER

"My flight is scheduled to come in tonight," Briana's voice came over the phone to Mark, "I booked my hotel room only for two nights. After that my boss expects me back at work."

Mark was silent at the other end. He heard Briana, but his thoughts had drifted elsewhere.

"Mark?" Briana's voice interrupted his thoughts.

"Yeah," Mark answered.

"Is there something wrong?" Briana asked.

"I'm thinking of telling my wife," Mark answered, "I think it might be time."

"Are you ready for it?" Briana asked.

"It is time she knew," Mark answered.

"We discussed this last time," Briana said, "Wait until you are ready before saying anything."

"You say anything to your boyfriend?" Mark asked.

"No," Briana answered, "And I'm not sure I ever will."

"I think it is time to tell me wife," Mark said.

Jackie was buzzing with happiness as she picked out the carrots she needed for tomorrow night's supper. She would be cooking for her parents and her husband. It was going to be a great occasion. Though it wouldn't be until tomorrow night that she found out why her parents decided to visit, but her mother had made it sound important. Immediately after the phone call was over Jackie had sat down and made up a plan for what would be for supper. Now she was buying everything for it.

Jackie saw Sara picking out bananas and remembered that she hadn't called Mark to tell him about her parents coming. Sara was Mark's sister-in-law and Jackie got along well with her.

"Hi," Jackie said stopping next to Sara.

"Hello," Sara said. She smiled at Jackie. "What are you doing here? I thought you only went shopping on Mondays."

"I usually do," Jackie answered, "But I'm buying things for supper tomorrow."

"What is happening?" Sara asked.

"My parents are coming to town for the night," Jackie answered, "Since Mark and I married three years ago this is the first time that I have gotten to cook for my parents."

"Isn't tomorrow the fifteenth?" Sara asked.

"Yes," Jackie answered, "Is there something about that date that is important?"

Sara seemed a little nervous now, as if she had assumed that Jackie should know something but wasn't sure if she should be the one to tell her.

"It is just that last year I was going to invite you and Mark to a gathering and I checked the date with Brandon," Sara said, "He said Mark was always busy on the fifteenth of October, every year. So I moved the party by one day and there wasn't a problem."

"I don't remember him being busy on that exact date, but he is busy with work so many days that it is hard to remember one specifically," Jackie said, "Did Brandon ever say why what Mark was busy that day?"

"No," Sara said, "When I asked he said he didn't know."

"I haven't spoken with Mark about supper yet," Jackie said, "I'll have to talk to him tonight. I'll see you later."

"See you," Sara said. She was still nervous as she left Jackie standing there. Jackie thought about it for a while as she finished shopping. She didn't remember Mark being busy exactly on October fifteenth. He never said anything about being busy on the fifteenth and he usually said something. Was this something she should be worried about? Should she confront him with what Sara told her? They were always honest with each other, so why wouldn't Mark tell her about the fifteenth?

Jackie had just put the casserole for supper into the oven when she heard the front door open and close. She glanced at the clock and saw that Mark wasn't supposed to be home for another half an hour.

"Hello?" Jackie called as she headed for the hallway.

"Hello," Mark's voice replied. She entered the hallway and saw him hanging up his overcoat. His briefcase and keys were sitting on the table in the hallway.

"Is there something wrong?" Jackie asked.

"No," Mark answered, "I just finished everything I had to do today and decided to come home rather than start something new."

"Okay," Jackie said. She went over and kissed him briefly on the lips. She was going to head back to the kitchen, but he wrapped his arms around her and held her close. She hugged him back, but she was confused as to what was going on with Mark. It took a minute before Mark let go. He brushed the hair out of her face. There was something in Mark's eyes that kept Jackie standing there when she might have otherwise gone back to the kitchen. She had never seen it before and she wasn't sure what it was.

"For several years I thought I would never find someone

I could love with all my heart," Mark said, "But I am glad you showed up in my life. You are the one person in this world I love with all my heart."

"I love you too," Jackie said. She could see that Mark was sincere, but she wasn't sure why he was saying this. Mark's cellphone went off before either of them could say anything. Mark sighed and took it out. He read the message on the screen.

"Something wrong?" Jackie asked.

"Nothing I can't deal with tomorrow," Mark answered as he closed his cellphone.

"My parents phoned earlier," Jackie said, "They are going to be coming through tomorrow night and I invited them for supper."

"Okay," Mark said. His face took on a thoughtful look, like he was trying to figure out something.

"I met Sara in the grocery store today," Jackie said. Jackie wanted to hesitate, but instead pressed on. "She said that you were always busy on the fifteenth of October."

"She's right," Mark said, "I usually take the fifteenth, but I don't have to be anywhere until quarter to six. That means I can be here for supper, but I will have to leave early."

"I'm sure that my parents won't mind if you have to leave early as long as you stay for supper," Jackie said. Mark didn't show anything that told Jackie what was going on in his head. She wanted to ask more about what Mark did on the fifteenth, but because this was the one thing Mark never talked about she was hesitated.

The microwave dinged from the kitchen. Jackie headed back into the kitchen to deal with it. Mark took his briefcase and headed toward his office.

Dinner with Jackie's parents was short because they wanted to visit some friends before the evening was over. They left by five-thirty and so neither Mark nor Jackie mentioned that Mark had to leave by quarter to six. In the middle of supper Mark's cellphone chirped, but out of respect for her parents he didn't leave the table to go check it. Jackie was thankfully for that, but it didn't cheer her up because he was still going off somewhere. When supper was finished Jackie's parents left. Mark helped Jackie fill the dishwasher. Jackie wondered if Mark could feel the tension that filled the silence or whether he was oblivious to it.

Jackie was standing in the dining room staring out the window at the dark. She could hear Mark as he checked his phone. It wasn't likely to be work, because no one from work ever phoned him this late in the day. It must be whoever he was going to meet. Mark moved from his office into the bedroom. Jackie knew he was getting his wallet and keys. She knew it was getting close to time for him to leave. It stung that he had never told her about this, but she was going to bury it. It would be better for her than overthinking it.

By the sounds of it Mark was now leaving the bedroom. She expected him to head toward the front door, but the sounds came toward the dining room. Jackie saw Mark come into the room in the reflection of the dining room window.

"It is time for me to head out," Mark said.

Jackie wanted to demand to know where he had to go, but instead she just nodded.

"Would you come with me?" Mark's voice had a pleading quality to it, like he wanted her to come but he was afraid she might get angry at him.

"Really?" Jackie was surprised. Her mood lifted a little. That was the last thing she expected him to say.

"Yes," Mark answered, "I want you to come."

"I need a couple minutes," Jackie said.

"That's okay," Mark said. Jackie went passed Mark and went to get her coat.

The happiness that had filled her dissipated a little when her mind started working on the idea. All the other things she thought he could be doing came back and with it how she might fit into it. But she grabbed her coat and purse. She put on her shoes and met Mark in the front entrance hall.

They left the house and Mark locked the door behind them. They got into Mark's car. Mark didn't say anything on the drive and Jackie didn't interrupt the quiet.

Mark pulled into a diner. It was older and Jackie wasn't sure she would have stopped there if she had just driven passed.

"We're going to stop here and have ice cream," Mark said, "I'll explain things. Then we will go somewhere else."

"Okay," Jackie said. Mark got out of the car and Jackie followed him out and into the diner. Mark went to the counter and ordered an ice cream sundae. The older man smiled and asked Mark how he was doing. Mark and old man seemed to know each other well. Jackie felt a little out of place, but she wasn't sure where to sit. The diner was full of vinyl booths and smelled of grease. There were only three groups of people sitting around the diner and all of them were under the age of twenty. All of that made Jackie uncomfortable, but Mark seemed right at home. The old man put the sundae on the counter with two spoons. Mark picked it up and went to a booth on the one side of the diner. It was away from the groups of teenagers, but that didn't seem to effect Mark's decision about where to sit. Mark set the sundae on the table before sitting down in the seat. Jackie slide onto the seat across from Mark.

"October fifteenth nineteen eighty-six I had supper at home with my parents," Mark said as he and Jackie started to eat the sundae, "After supper I went out. Mia and I had a date planned, but I didn't tell my parents I was going out with her. They didn't think I should go out with her. We met here at six o'clock."

Jackie glanced at over stylized clock on the wall and saw it was a couple minutes after six. She didn't remember anyone ever talking about a Mia in Mark's past.

"We shared an ice cream sundae," Mark continued, "We sat and talked for half an hour at least. It was just a regular date night for us. When we finished we walked down the street to the park. It was a nice night for a walk. At the park we stopped at a bench and I got down on one knee. I asked her to marry me."

Mark was quiet for a second. Jackie waited for him to finish the story.

"She said yes. We were both very happy and wanted to celebrate," Mark finally continued, "But there was no point in going home to tell our parents. Hers didn't care and mine didn't want us dating. So from the park we headed into town. We met up with Will and Briana at Fourth and Baker. They were out on a date as well. We told them the big news and both were excited for us. The four of us went to the Crymsym Bar. We had to sneak in at the time, but that didn't matter to us. At seventeen it was part of the thrill. We had a drink there before we left. We weren't interested in getting drunk, just celebrating. From there the four of us took Will's car up to the lookout point.

"It was beautiful up there. It was a little cold, but we sat there talking for half an hour or more. Finally it was getting late so we climbed back into Will's car and headed back down the road. There was loose gravel on the road. Will wasn't going very fast when he hit the loose gravel, but it was fast enough. He lost control of the car and it went through the guard rail. I don't remember what happened next. Either my memory blocks it out, or I hit my head. I woke up lying on the steep embankment slightly above where the car was now lying on its roof. Briana had dragged me there. Will and Mia were still in the car. Sitting up made me dizzy so I lay there while Briana went back into the car and pulled Will out. I had been closest and now

Will was the closest. She dragged him up the slope to where I was before going back for Mia. I checked his pulse, but couldn't find one. Somehow I thought maybe I was doing it wrong, because Will couldn't be dead.

"Briana pulled out Mia and dragged her up the slope before collapsing on to the ground. I checked Mia's pulse and found one, or at least I thought I had. I'm not sure anymore. Briana sat there as if she was unsure what to do. I got to my feet. I was dizzy, but I didn't let that stop me. I started to climb back up to the road. It seemed to take forever before I reached it. Then I went along the road until I found the emergency telephone. I used it to call for help. I sat down to wait for the police to arrive and the next thing I remember was being transported to the hospital in the ambulance. I tried to tell them about the car, but was told that it had been found and another ambulance was there.

"My parents came and got me when I was released, but no one would tell me anything about Mia, Will or Briana. It wasn't until the next day when I read in the newspaper. Mia and Will had died. Briana was still alive. I locked myself in my room and spent the day crying. Other than that there wasn't much emotion I could show over the incident. My parents gave me a lecture on being around people they disapproved of and then pretended it never happened."

The sundae was finished. Mark and Jackie put the spoons into the dish. Mark got up and Jackie followed him. They left the diner, but Mark didn't go to the car. Instead he headed for the park down the street. Jackie followed him.

"October fifteenth nineteen eighty-seven, I went out in a depressed mood. I found myself at the diner for a sundae. When I left the diner and walked to the park. I sat there for a while before heading into town," Mark started his story again, "I met Briana at the corner of Fourth and Baker. We went to the Crymsyn bar for a drink before going up to the lookout. We sat there and talked about Mia and Will. While up there we decided to meet every year on October fifteenth to remember the ones we lost. And that is what I've been doing on the fifteenth of October. That is the reason I'm always busy on that day."

Mark and Jackie reached the park. He sat down on a bench and she sat down beside her.

"When I asked Mia to marry me I thought she was my soul mate and there was no one else out there for me," Mark said, "But I was proven wrong. I lost Mia, but I found someone I love even more." Mark smiled at Jackie. Jackie smiled back at him. He leaned over and placed a gentle kiss on her lips.

Fourth and Baker was lit with light from shop signs and street lights. Brief periods of darkness came between the headlights of the cars going passed. There were a few people out and about. Some people shopping, some out on dates, and the occasional lost soul who hadn't found a shelter for the night. Jackie held on to Mark's hand. She was glad he had told her about Mia and let her come along for the rest of the night. She didn't remember anyone ever mentioning Mia or the car accident, but they might not see any reason to bring it up.

There was only one person at Fourth and Baker who was not going anywhere was a lady. She wore a pair of tight blue jeans, a black leather jacket, and red shirt. Her dark brown hair was braided. Jackie also noticed a tattoo peaked above the collar of her shirt. The type of person she looked like was not the type of person Mark usually spent time with.

The lady smiled when she saw them coming. Mark and Jackie stopped in front of her.

"Briana, this is my wife Jackie," Mark said, "Jackie, this is Briana."

"Nice to meet you," Briana held out her hand.

"Nice to meet you too," Jackie shook the offered hand.

"The Crymsyn Bar is a little busy tonight," Briana said as they started down the street toward the red neon sign in the shape of a dress, "But I made a reservation for a table."

"Okay," Mark said, "How was your flight?"

"It was okay," Briana answered, "I didn't have to make the extra stopover this time, but the hotel room was not the one I usually book. The room I usually book has a view of the city, but the one I got this time faces a building. Hopefully they'll let me book my usual room for next year before I leave. How have you been?"

"Good," Mark answered, "I got a promotion a couple months ago and now my cellphone rings at all hours, except when I'm in the office where they can find me."

"It pays better, right?" Briana asked.

"Yeah," Mark answered, "And it is more interesting. I just like to have evenings and weekends off. So far I have managed to avoid actually going into the office when they call me."

"That is good," Briana said.

"How are things with your boyfriend?" Mark asked.

"We were doing fine until a couple days ago," Briana answered.

"Then you got a plane for a mysterious trip?" Mark asked.

"Actually the fight was before that," Briana answered, "He thinks I left to get some space. No, the fight had more to do with his mother. She wants him to get married sooner than later. So, he wants to skip the engagement and all that to go straight to a courthouse wedding. I told him no and he got upset with me."

"Sounds like this relationship is over," Mark said.

"I didn't want it to be," Briana said, "But I think I will get to go back to pack my stuff and leave. I'm still thinking it over. It is at times like these that I miss Will the most."

They reached the Crymsyn bar and went inside. Briana identified herself to the host and he showed them to a table near the back where it was quiet. The server came over and they each ordered a drink. Briana ordered whiskey, Mark ordered rum and coke, and Jackie ordered white wine.

"Will gave me this class ring at the beginning of the year," Briana said, "We hadn't been dating very long at that point, but he told me that a week after graduating he would give me a real ring."

"I gave Mia my class ring as an engagement ring," Mark said, "I apologized for not being able to afford a proper ring, but she didn't care."

"I guess first loves are like that," Briana said. The server brought their drinks. After checking to make sure they didn't need anything else, the server left them alone. Briana picked up her glass and raised it for a toast. Mark and Jackie did the same.

"Happiness," Briana said. The three of them touched glasses and then drank.

They finished the drinks in quiet. Briana left the money on the table with a sizeable tip before they left. They walked back to Mark's car.

Jackie wasn't paying attention to where the car was going until Mark pulled into a parking space at the base of the road up to the lookout. Mark turned the engine off and all three of them got out. They started up the road to the lookout.

"The one difference between that night and now," Mark said, "Is that we don't drive up there."

"The police figured it was just an accident," Briana said, "And the roads have been kept cleaner since then. But we don't want to tempt fate."

Jackie nodded.

Once at the top they sat there and talked for a while before heading back down. Mark dropped Briana off at her hotel before heading home.

Jackie crawled into bed. Mark was already there. He turned off the lamp near him as she pulled the covers up. They laid there is the quiet for several minutes before Jackie draped her arm over Mark and put her head on his chest.

"Thank you for letting me in," Jackie said.

The Best Brownie Recipe

B. Heather Mantler

THE DOOR

Charlotte wandered down the street. She was on her way to work, but she was half an hour early so she did not feel the urgency of normal. She did this on occasion just to have a chance to see the neighbour rather than rush by it. This helped her feel relaxed and let her notice things. Like the different fruits the street vendor was selling today, or the flowers blooming in the window boxes.

Something caught Charlotte's attention and she stopped. This wall had been covered with graffiti yesterday when she went passed and today it had been repainted a cream. But that wasn't the surprising part. It was the door that had not been there before now in the middle of the wall. Whoever had put it in had put it in quickly and made sure that it looked like it had always been there. If Charlotte had not been paying attention she would have missed that the door was new.

The door itself was built from several long boards held together with four short boards, which were equal distance apart with the first at the top of the door and the last at the bottom. There were no cracks in the door, but there was a metal doorknob and deadbolt. The door was painted a dark red.

Charlotte just stood there and looked at the door. It was a strange door compared to the metal and glass doors on every other building. This made Charlotte curious about the door. She had been standing there for a few minutes when someone stopped beside her. Charlotte glanced at the person out of the corner of her eye. It was a woman in a white blazer, dark blue jeans, and forest green shirt. Her black hair was loosely pulled back in a clip.

"It is a strange looking door, isn't it?" her voice deeper than Charlotte expected.

"It wasn't there yesterday," Charlotte said, "Or at least, I don't remember seeing it. I wonder where it goes."

"A basement, maybe?" the woman said, "Or perhaps for janitors?"

"The building has a level of underground parking," Charlotte said, "The entrance to that is in the alley way along with the back door to the building, which is used by the janitors. Everyone else uses the front door, which is on the other side of the building. It is an office building, so there isn't any reason for another one on this side."

"Perhaps they needed another door to the parking lot," the woman said.

"I don't think so," Charlotte shook her head, "The door must lead to something else."

"Where do you think the door leads?" the woman asked.

"With the way the door is built," Charlotte answered, "It looks like it should lead someplace magical."

"Like in all those fantasy books," the woman sounded like she smiled at the suggestion, "Where they step through a door and find themselves in a medieval time where there is a princess who needs saving, but first they have to meet the master who is going to teach them the ways of this new and strange world."

"And they end up leading a party with a magical creature like a dragon and elves," Charlotte smiled, "And they get the princess in the end because they want to stay in that world."

"Maybe the door just leads to the fairy nest," the woman said, "Where they take the person prisoner until they find out the person isn't a danger to them."

"And then the fairies need someone to help them with something that involves going into human society," Charlotte said, "But one fairy won't let the person go alone."

"The fairy is friendly and helpful," the woman said, "But her magic is weak compared to all other fairies and she needs the person's help to discover why."

"Or maybe the door leads to a settlement on the edge of the ocean," Charlotte said, "And after the person goes through the pirate ship attacks. They get taken as a hostage on board the ship, where slowly they work their way into the captain's confidences and he doesn't kill the person as he had intended."

"The person ends up adventuring with the crew for a while," the woman said, "Until they attack the ship with the gorgeous woman who needs help against the pirates. Then the person saves the woman and returns her home, where he finds out that she is a princess."

"The king is willing to give him a chest of gold for his efforts," Charlotte said, "But the princess has already fallen in love with him."

"And she refused to marry anyone else," the woman said, "So they run off to sea together."

"Or stepping through the door could put the person in the barracks in a world war two prisoner of war camp," Charlotte said, "The British soldiers are getting their escape plan ready."

"They let the person join because being from this time they provide some help to the escape plan," the woman said, "And having studied history, the person knows what is happening in Germany at that time and the best routes out of Germany."

"This information saves all their lives as they make their way to safety," Charlotte said, "They find a plane they steal has secret papers inside which were destined for the German high command, but are now headed back with the British Soldiers."

"The person has a drink with the soldiers in an English pub," the woman said, "And he leaves the pub alone to find himself back on this street, where everything is back to normal. He shakes his head and goes back to his life with a new sense of things."

"The other side of the door could be the future," Charlotte said, "Where there are colonies on the moon and ships that travel across galaxies in minutes. Humans have started replacing parts that break down with new machine ones."

"And they find themselves far more machine," the woman said, "The person is the last pure human and is the only one left who can teach people what it means to be human.'

"But the man who owns the company that makes the machine parts doesn't want people to go back to being human," Charlotte said, "Because if they do, they would start refusing his parts, which means he would lose money. With the loss of money is the loss of the power he enjoys too much."

"But humanity spreads faster than either the owner of the company or the person who stepped through the door realizes," the woman said, "And the people make the decision for themselves. They get rid of the machine parts to go back to being human."

"Maybe the door goes to a basement under the parking lot," Charlotte said, "After bumping around because of the darkness the person finds a stone door. This door leads into an old musty tomb."

"Down here a statue on one of the stone caskets comes

to life with the spirit of the man laying below the lid," the woman said, "The spirit needs some help before it can rest."

"The person was murdered," Charlotte said, "And you have to figure out who killed them and why."

"To figure it out the person has to go back in records from a century before," the woman said, "While doing research in old and dusty places, the person finds themselves in danger from something that doesn't want the mystery solved."

"Eventually the person finds the living relative of the man who had been murdered, but didn't want the family history to come out because of the scandal," Charlotte said, "Because the murderer was the man's brother who was having an affair with his wife which had produced a child. This child couldn't be passed off as anyone else because of the markings the child shares with his father."

"The father had been banned from having any relationships because people thought the markings showed him to be the result of a curse on the family," the woman said, "The victim would have had to kill his brother when he found out. She should have killed herself as soon as she found out she was pregnant. But because the son was born, she instead hid the markings and lied to protect the family."

"The spirit can rest now that he has the answers, but he didn't like them," Charlotte said, "Or the door could just be them doing renovations on the building and the door is for the janitors. Thanks." Charlotte smiled at the woman.

"You're welcome," the woman smiled back. Charlotte continued down the street toward her work place.

The woman watched Charlotte until she was around the corner and out of sight. The woman went to the door and opened it. She stepped on to the dirt steps and closed the door behind her.

BITTER REVENGE

The man placed the papers in his briefcase and snapped it shut before shaking the client's hand. Then the client's assistant showed him out. He walked to the corner and stopped to wait for the light.

On the far corner a father was buying ice cream for his son. The little boy's face shone with happiness as ice cream dribbled down his chin.

The man crossed the other way to get to the opposite corner as if the father and son had some contagious disease. He continued down the street.

There were noises coming from downstairs. The boy crept to the top stair and looked down at the scene below. His father was sitting just inside the front door, laughing. His mother was a silent shadow watching from the living room with tears streaming down her face, scared to move.

Across the street was the police station. A teenaged boy was being dragged out of a police car as a woman with tear-stained face came running. The man looked away before the woman reached the teenager. He didn't want to see the further tears or the hug or the officer trying to get the woman to let go.

The boy ran up the steps into the house. He was practically whistling over the baseball practice. The boy skidded to a halt when his father came out of the kitchen, all happiness forgotten.

"There you are, boy," his father said.

"I have homework to do," the boy started toward the stairs.

"Forget it for now," his father said, "I have something more important for you to do."

The boy turned back to his father as his stomach started to hurt.

"It is time for you to pull your own weight," his father said, "I've feed you and paid for this roof over your head for twelve years. Now I got you a job, so that you can do your part."

"But," the boy started.

"Be ready to go in an hour," his father turned and went back into the kitchen. The boy saw his mother sitting at the kitchen table. She turned away as her husband came toward her.

The man pushed the memory away and kept walking. Reaching the next corner he found a road construction crew had set up and was blocking him from just crossing straight to the corner he needed. He crossed the other way to go around the crew. As he reached the third corner two boys went passed on skateboards. They were racing each other.

The truck pulled into the parking lot of the bar, the place his father drank himself into the state that scared his mother. His father parked out front. The sign telling you the name of the bar lit up the whole front, but the neon sign to say it was open was dark. His father turned off the trunk.

"Come on, boy," his father opened the door and climbed out. The boy opened his door and climbed down before following his father around the back. His father knocked on the kitchen door. The door opened and the doorway was filled with a man who made his father look small in size.

His father, who was always the tallest, the broadest and the most solid, was small.

"This is Robert," his father told the man. The man nodded.

"Since you're here, Kid, you might as well come in and get started," the man said to the boy. His father turned and left. The boy was shown to a sink full of dirty dishes. The boy bowed his head and got started.

The man blinked as if to adjust to bright sunshine despite the layers of clouds hiding it. He crossed the street to the corner he wanted. Going up the steps to the office building he went inside. The man went up to his office on the third floor by the elevator.

Entering the office he went over to his desk chair. He stopped before sitting down and stared out the window.

This was his fourth year standing at this sink paying off his father's bar tab. Of course he had figured out how much he needed to work to get money for himself. He hid it from his father and counted it every night. The amount was at the top his head because he was sure he had enough to get out of this kitchen.

Jack dumped more dishes into the sink on his way passed. The gray water was splashed down the young man's front.

"Your father has gone home," Jack called back as he opened the door to the cooler. The young man nodded knowing he could now go home in an hour. Go home to collect his stuff and leave again. Jack went passed again, this time carrying two cases of liquor.

The young man had worked for half an hour when Jack came into the back with a police officer following him. Once the officer saw the young man, Jack turned around and went back out front.

The officer told the young man about his father driving his truck into a semi, which tried to avoid him and ended up sending both vehicles crashing into the river. A stranger's voice asked, that might have come from the young man, about the semi's driver. The officer said the semi driver was fine. The young man nodded and was led out of the bar by the officer.

The young man stared out the window of the police car as the officer went around to the driver's side. The neon lights were the only thing the young man could see. And those lights became everything the boy hated.

I will be back, the young man swore, and when I do I will burn this place to cinders.

"Robert," a voice interrupted. The man turned around. The boss's assistant stood on the doorway.

"Mr. Randall would like to speak with you," the assistant said.

"I will be right up," the man said. The assistant nodded and left. The man took a deep breath and headed up to the next floor where his boss's office was.

The door was open as an invitation to enter. His boss stood by the window as if in contemplation. The man stayed outside the office and knocked on the door. His boss turned around.

"Robert, come in," Mr. Randall said. The man stepped into the office. "Close to door behind you."

The man did as he was told. His boss signaled for him to sit down before sitting down in his own chair. The man sat down.

"I received a letter from your staff," his boss looked down at a piece of paper on his desk before looking back up at the man, "They are worried about you. It says that you seem to be." His boss stopped as if searching for the right phrase.

"Somewhere else," the man supplied.

"Yes," Mr. Randall said.

"I apologize for the effects of my behaviour. And I am sorry it got bad enough my staff felt it necessary to talk to you," the man said. His boss waited for the rest of it.

"I talked to my mother last week," the lie came as smooth as if he had been practicing it for years, "And some things she said has me worried, even though she claims to be fine."

"Does you mother live in town?" Mr. Randall asked.

"No, she lives in Birch Creek," the man answered.

"Why don't you take a few days off to go visit her? Then you can make sure everything is fine," Mr. Randall said, "take as long as you need."

"Are you sure?" the man asked.

"You have worked for this company for ten years," Mr. Randall said, "and have never taken a sick day or vacation. We will do fine for the few days that you will be gone."

"Thank you, sir," the man said.

"I find it better when my employees can concentrate on their work," his boss's attention drifted to papers on his desk.

"Yes, sir," the man stood up. He left the office and went back to his own.

The man woke up when his head banged against the window as the bus make a tight corner. He straightened up and felt a sharp pain in his neck. It almost sent him cursing the situation, but he remembered it was his choice to take the bus when he could have afforded to travel any way he wanted.

The man managed to brace himself as the bus took another tight corner. Looking out the window the man saw that they were in Birch Creek. He might not recognize most of the people, but the town itself hadn't changed. The man got ready to get off.

The young man climbed aboard the bus and went all the way to the back. No one gave him a second glance. Once in his seat, the young man looked out the window. His mother still stood in the same place as he had hugged her a moment ago. She had brought him a ticket, even though the young man knew she didn't want to lose her son so soon after losing her husband. The young man didn't understand why she still loved the man that his father had been.

The bus started and pulled out of the station. The young man watched his mother as she wiped her face. She had kept control until she had thought he couldn't see her.

Maybe I should at least stop in and see my mother while I'm here, the man thought as the bus pulled into the station. The man picked up his bag and got off the bus. He was the only one to get off at this stop. Once he was clear the door closed and the bus headed off to its next stop.

The man started in the direction of the bar. No one seemed to recognize him, which he didn't mind. His mind worked on how to burn the place down. He would probably have to buy the property to avoid a charge of arson. But that was okay he had the money saved up. Would it be a good idea to call the fire department to let them know what he was doing? Would they let him burn the bar? How would it be best to burn a building to nothing but ashes? Gasoline? Kindling and a match?

The man left most of the city behind him. Around the next bend in the road was the bar, in its little alcove off the highway. Many people had missed it the first couple times because if you didn't know where it was you would go right passed the turn off.

After the bend the man could see the access road. Trees and bushes had grown up at the edge of the highway making is difficult to see the bar. As the man continued something started to feel wrong. Why would Jack let trees hinder the view of the neon signs he never turned off?

The view through the trees became clearer and where the neon lights should have been was empty space. The man started to run. He stopped when he reached the space where the bar had once stood. In its place were an outline of a structure, a pile of battered wood and other scrapes of junk. The man collapsed to his knees. The sobs wracked his whole body as he stared at the rubble in despair. Everything that was his life was gone.

B. Heather Mantler

A COACH RIDE

The coach pulled up to the porch. The coach was black and shiny in the places where the moonlight touched it. The blackness of the horses absorbed the light and made them hard to see. The driver sat high in the seat with a rain coat that blended in with the coach so it was hard to tell where the coat ended and the coach began.

Slowly the driver turned his head toward me. Instead of a face looking back at me, there was a shadow of a white skull. The light didn't touch it.

"Come up," the deep voice invited as the door to the coach opened with a creak. I looked back at the dark ticket station. The person who sold me the ticket had gone home hours ago. All he said before he left was for me to wait until my coach arrived. I was sure this wasn't it.

I looked at my ticket in the light of the single lit lantern. The time was right, but I am sure this isn't my coach.

"Come up," the deep voice invited again.

I didn't know what else to do so I picked up my bag and climbed inside. I sat down on the right seat as close to the door as possible. I put my bag next to me on the seat. The door closed after me with a creak and thud.

Inside the coach it would have been pitch black, except the curtain on the other side of the coach was open and letting the moonlight shine in. In that moonlight I could see the outline of the other passenger in the coach. It was a skeleton in a black and white dress suit. The eyeless sockets appeared to look back at me and cause the skeleton to grin.

I reached for the door handle, but I could not find one. The coach started to move, pushing me back in the seat.

"You can't get off once you get on," the voice was a normal tone, but had an echo quality to it. I glanced at the skeleton. He just grinned back.

The coach sped up with the howling of a pack of wolves. I pulled myself into the corner and tried to ignore the fear icing my spine. I closed my eyes and wished myself somewhere else, anywhere else.

A moaning caused me to open my eyes again, but I really should have kept them close. It was not my fellow passenger, but a woman I could see outside the coach window. She was flying alongside the coach and moaning. I could make out every detail of her face and clothes, but I could also see the blur of the scenery through her.

I searched for the door handle; not only with my eyes but with my fingers as well. There was nothing there. I sat back. My companion appeared to be close to laughter. I got up and pushed the curtain with the thought of screaming for help. Instead I was face to face with the ghostly image of Finny. I screamed and jerked the curtains shut.

"You're guilty," the voice bounced around the coach before it reached me. I felt like fingers were grasping in the darkness for me as I stumbled back into the seat.

"I didn't do it," I cried, "I didn't do it." The darkness just got closer. The other passenger smirked at me with a know-it-all expression before it disappeared into the dark.

"I didn't do it," I screamed, "I didn't do it."

The darkness blinded me, choked me, and suffocated

me. I clawed at the air in front of me, but there was nothing there to fight. My throat tightened further and my chest felt compressed. I could not get any air in.

Guilty. The word echoed in my head. I tried to deny it, but the words could not form. The word repeated several times as I collapsed on to the seat. My flaying hands dropped down as I ran out of energy to keep trying to escape this horror. The lack of air was having its effect. And then I blacked out.

Somehow I found myself taking breathes. The air tasted musty but I ignored that and just took in big gulps. Wherever I was, it was so dark I couldn't tell when my eyes were open or closed. It was an enclosed space because I was lying on my back and there was something fairly close in front of me. I felt around until I found my pocket and took out my matches. Fumbling around for several minutes I finally got one lit. I could see the wood in front of me as well as some to my left. I turned to my right and between me and the wood was Finny's body. The corpse smiled at me through the decay of death. Then the match went out. I screamed but there was no way for anyone to hear me.

NOTES

The narrator's gender is not mentioned in the story (In Need of a White Christmas) and for the point of the story it is unnecessary. However, in my head the narrator has always been male. I do not know why.

IN NEED OF A WHITE CHRISTMAS

At home we went inside. It was quiet inside. The same quiet we had left this morning. I hung up my coat before turning on the living room light. The Christmas tree lights came on at the same time. The multi-coloured lights that should have brought the usual joy of years past left me feeling depressed instead. We have put the tree up earlier this week. It had been an attempt to distract from thoughts of Mom and how sick she is. Most of the rest of the Christmas decorations were still packed away. I couldn't stand to put anything else up. Shopping this year was a similar experience. Every time I went into a store playing carols I wanted to scream. How am I supposed to be jolly when my mother is lying in a care home waiting to die? There were still some presents for each of us from various relatives who always sent a gift. Those went under the tree along with the box containing the ever growing stack of unopened Christmas cards from people I don't even recognize the names of anymore.

Mom had been the holiday person when I was growing up. If it had been up to Dad we would have had a tree with a few ornaments, one gift each, and turkey without all the fuss. But every year the house was decorated top to bottom, the tree was bursting with ornaments, there were gifts for anyone who cared to show up at our door, and the turkey was surrounded by heaping dishfuls of everything. But Mom never thought Christmas was truly right without snow. One year the four of us siblings got our money together and send Mom and Dad off to somewhere warm for Christmas. When Mom got back she announced she would rather stay home for Christmas, because it didn't feel like Christmas with sand instead of snow.

I closed the curtains against the stark, brown landscape that lay just beyond the walls of the house. The weather report for this morning had been rain for today and tomorrow and into next week. I didn't mind too much, it matched my mood. But it was another reason why it didn't feel like Christmas.

Supper was quiet. What was there to say? The doctors were sure she would die in the next few days. The weather was bleak. It was Christmas tomorrow, but we have already turned down all the invitations that had come. What more is there to talk about?

Bedtime was a relief in not having to worry about what to say. After an hour I was the only one wake. I got up and went to the window. The storm clouds had gathered outside. The leaves were brown and lying limp on the lawn. The trees in the yard all had bare branches. The streetlights showed the same scene played out on the rest of the street. Lots of the houses had Christmas lights up in designs. They were reflected off the roof of the car making them into burs. Lights in most of the houses were turned off and some of the cars that had been there when we had come home were gone. The parties were over and everyone was asleep waiting for Santa Claus to come and deliver the rest of the gifts.

Every year until I was a teenager I stayed up half the night listening for Santa Claus. And I was always the first one up in the morning. Mom always took a picture at ten o'clock in the morning of me lying on the couch surrounded by my gifts. I was always asleep. If put all together in one album it would have shown you how much changed between years, like a school photo would. Now I stand here, not waiting on Santa Claus, but waiting to see if the phone call would come tonight or whether Mom would live until Christmas.

It was only a couple minutes until midnight when the phone broke the silence that had filled the house for the last couple weeks. I let the curtain fall over my view of the window and went over to pick it up. It was the doctor and the news was what I was expecting. She had died a moment ago. Died before she could see another Christmas. The doctor said I could come in on the twenty-seventh to go over whatever plans needed to be made. I said that was fine. He paused. I waited in the usual silence of expecting something else to go bad.

"Your mother said something before she died. She said that it would be Christmas and you would know. And she hoped you would at least be happy it was Christmas."

"I wish I could be happy about that. But it isn't Christmas without snow."

The doctor said good night. I placed the receiver back in its spot and related the news to the open pair of eyes on the other side of the bed from me. The gentle hand reached over and squeezed my hand. Then it was silent for a while. Finally I was once again the only one awake.

Standing up I went back to the window and pulled back the curtain. The multi-coloured lights were still on, but they were much brighter. The brown leaves had disappeared, the branches were no longer bare, and I couldn't see anything reflected on the roof of the car. It was all being covered by the falling snow.

CLIFF HANGER

"So there I was hanging from a rope, which was about to break, over the side of the cliff. And I thought to myself, okay, how are you going to get out of this one?" The guy made himself more comfortable on the bar stool. He took a sip of his half-full beer. He was preparing himself to tell the story and the group of the guys around the bar prepared themselves to listen.

"I guess I should start at the beginning," the guy licked the beer off his lips, "I was working for CSIS. Of course, I can't tell you the exact position I held, or even the nature of the work. That day I had been sent into the Rocky Mountains to investigate an American intelligence base. We had known about it since they snuck in to build it, but my superiors hadn't been bothered with it until then."

"I left civilization behind at Fernie, BC and headed north into conifer forests and steep terrain," the guy continued after some more beer, "Let me tell you, there isn't much out there that is friendly. But I knew how to handle the animals and even the patrols that got between me and my destination."

The guy took another gulp of beer and leaned toward his

audience.

"I was a couple hours into the bush when I encountered my first patrol. There were four of them in camo. They almost looked like hunters, except they moved with the precision that comes from boot camp. At the first sound of human movement I had dropped to my stomach behind some brush. Each member of the patrol swung their heads back and forth looking for upright violations of security. Once they had stalked by, I moved into a crouch and started to follow. The last man in line must have assumed the noise was nothing important because he didn't even bother to glance over his shoulder.

"As I straightened up, I brought his gun up to his throat. He made a gurgling sound as I cut off his air supply. The idiots in front didn't notice and kept going. I pulled the man into the brush by his throat. He was unconscious, but I didn't want to take any chances so I used his knife to slit his throat. I wiped off the blood on his jacket before following the rest of the patrol."

The guy finished his beer and signal for another one. He didn't say anything until the bartender had finished with what he was doing, had wandered down to the guy and poured another beer. The guy took a sip as if making sure it was the correct drink. Only once satisfied did he start again.

"When I caught up to the next member of the patrol, he glanced back briefly. I acted like the person who was supposed to be behind him and he turned back around. By the time it registered who was there, I had the blade going across his neck. He didn't make any noise as I dragged him into the bush.

"But something had tipped off the other two because they had found a clear area and were standing back to back with their guns at ready. I watched them from my position lying behind a bush. They were going around in a slow circle as they tried to defend from all directions at once."

The guy stopped the story long enough to take a couple

gulps of his beer. When he was satisfied, he started telling the story.

"I don't know what it was, but their spinning was making me dizzy. I closed my eyes and lay my head down for a moment, which helped briefly. I looked at them again and felt bile rising in my throat. Putting my head down, I got the knife ready. Then I glanced up long enough to sight my target and throw the knife. After the two thuds, I was going to check the situation but the spray of bullets above me caused me to cover my head and stay down.

"I waited until there was a break in the gunfire before looking up. One of the men was lying on the ground with the knife embedded in his chest and the other was reloading his weapon. I rolled to the left instead of into the tree on my right. I flattened out as the bullets started again. The man hadn't changed his aim."

The guy stopped his story to drink the top half of his beer. He licked it from his lips before continuing.

"Again I waited until he ran out of bullets. But this time I took that pause to rush the man. I slammed into his stomach, which knocked the gun one direction while he went the other. With him down, I used both hands clasped together to hit him several times. When he stopped fighting, I used his side-arm to finish the job.

"I continued up the mountain. Over the next ten hours, I hiked deep into those woods and took out patrols about hourly. All the patrols were dealt with in a similar method to the first one, but I managed to deal with them without any more shots fired. After that it changed to a patrol every half an hour for the next six hours. Here's a hint, the more enemy patrols there are the closer you are to the enemy base."

The guy finished off his beer and signalled for another. The bartender has been caught up in the story and so was there to get the refill. The guy took a gulp of the beer.

"The opening of the base was on the top of that

particular mountain. It was hidden beneath a large shrub, but there were enough scuff marks in the dirt to tell where it was. The opening was a solid, metal manhole. I started out checking for traps, just in case. There were none, or even alarms. I opened the manhole and slipped inside. There was a metal ladder that went down to a tunnel. The only light until I reached the tunnel was the sunlight coming in through the hole. In the tunnel there were lights along the wall to my right. There were no enemies in the tunnel. The tunnel itself was made of concrete and there was a door at each end.

"I stood and listened, but aside from a steady electrical hum there was nothing. If I remembered my orders correctly I was to go to the right. I proceeded to do so. The door at the end of the tunnel opened to a staircase which spiralled down to the next tunnel. I went down the metal stairs. At the bottom was another door, which opened into another tunnel. This one was made of metal and had doors along both sides. Each door had a small window in the door. I peered in the window of the first one. It was a small room with a bed, but otherwise empty.

"I continued down this hallway to the end, which had another door with a staircase on the other side. It was a few levels down that was my destination. The third tunnel had rooms on both sides with closed doors and large windows beside the doors instead of in them. The windows were dark like they were the other side of two-way mirrors. All the rooms were empty when I looked inside.

"The tunnel I was looking for had one door in the middle of each side. The door on the left side was closed, but door on the right side was open. I checked the room out from my position beside the door. There was a man sitting at a computer in a room full of work stations. He was wearing headphones. I stepped into the room without him noticing me until I had the cord around his neck. He choked for a moment before passing out and I let him slip out of the chair to the floor.

"I looked at the computers until I found the station I had been instructed to use. I plugged the jump drive into the computer. Once the computer had acknowledged it, I found the files needed and saved them. It took several minutes to download, but no one came into the room. Finally it finished and I was able to take the drive out of the computer."

The guy stopped for another couple gulps of beer. The patrons of the bar waited for him. Even the sound of the sports channel had been muted to hear him better. He took another mouthful and swallowed before starting again.

"I turned to leave the room and didn't see the man on the floor move. He pressed a button and suddenly alarms were going. I didn't bother with him as he had already done damage to my mission and I needed to exit. I ran through the tunnels and took the stairs several at a time. I was in the second tunnel before enemies were coming at me.

"There were six in the first group. They didn't shoot and had batons out. The first man swung his baton and I ducked before coming up under his arm. I slammed him hard against wall of the tunnel. He collapsed to the floor and didn't get up. The second and third man came at me at once despite the size of the tunnel. I blocked the first baton with my right forearm and put my left elbow into his stomach while dodging the second baton. The man who got the elbow in the stomach bent over in pain and I shoved him into the other man. They got tangled up and I hit their heads together. They both found the floor.

"I stepped over them and into the next man. I blocked his baton with my left arm before punching him with my right hand. He moved to headbutt me, but I went right. This left me open to the man behind him, who slammed his baton into my side. I collapsed enough to get below him. He swung the baton and I moved upward with my whole body. I sent him into the metal wall. He didn't hit his head and was shaking it off as the man on my left was coming with his baton.

"I stepped back at the last second and his baton hit the man who was recovering. He barely held back as to not do serious injury. I dodged both and tackled the final man. He slammed into the floor and I headed for the door to the staircase. I could hear the other two climbing over their fallen patrol member. I was going two stairs at a time before they could get through."

The guy stopped again for a few sips of his beer. He stopped with a little bit left in his glass, looked at it and then poured the rest down his throat. The bartender didn't need to be signalled to get another beer. The guy waited until the glass was set in front of him. He took a sip, looked around at his audience, and then went back into the story.

"At the top of the stairs were two more men. Before they could start swinging, I grabbed the closest one and tossed him down the stairs. The second man grabbed my jacket and I used my weight to smack him into the wall. Then I sent him after his buddy and down the stairs. I slammed the door shut and headed for the ladder out of the base.

"At the top of the ladder, I looked and saw more patrols coming towards me through the trees. None were close enough for combat. I crawled out and stayed low to the ground. There was some bush for cover. An opening in the patrols to the north. I headed there. I started out crawling, but wasn't fast enough so I moved to a crouch. As the brush thinned out to nothing, I started running. There was a shout, which let me know the patrols were coming after me.

"Apparently there was a reason no one was coming from the north. The ground turned to a slope quickly and then got steep. My foot hit a rock and I went sprawling, which changed into a roll. This might have gotten me further from the patrols than running, I don't know. Next thing I did know there was a cliff edge and a rope hanging over it. I managed to wrap my hand in the rope as I went over. My hand slid along the rope until a knot stopped my progress.

"Now I was hanging quite a distance from the ground by one hand. I heard the rope scrap against the rock above me. I looked up to see the rope was rubbing against a sharp rock, which was doing damage with my swinging. I had no idea how far behind me the patrols were, but they aren't going to matter soon if I didn't get myself out of this sticky situation."

The guy's cellphone rang. He took it out and looked at the display.

"Excuse me," the guy said, "It is work calling and I have to go." He finished his drink in a quick succession of gulps before getting off his stool. He strode out of the bar and was gone.

NOTES

The inspiration for Innocence Hung came from the song The Hanging Tree written by Suzanne Collins for her book Mockingjay(2010) and was then performed by Jennifer Lawrence in The Hunger Games: Mockingjay-Part 1(2014).

INNOCENCE HUNG

Grace shivered against the cold of the darkness which had settled over the forest just moments before with the sunset. Her mother had always encouraged her to be home before dark and Grace had always listened, except tonight when she had lost track of time in town and didn't head back to the farm soon enough. She was lucky she had her lantern with her for light, however right at this moment Grace felt as if it was not enough.

Just head was the intersection of three paths where there were large oak trees between them. There was the sound of something heavy swinging in the wind. Grace lifted her lantern and it settled on a man hanging from the closest oak, which had a branch hanging out over the path. There was no doubt that he was dead.

"Come to meet your lover?" the female voice came from behind Grace. Grace spun around and shone her lantern in front of her. The lady standing appeared real enough with her grey hair pulled back and a shawl over a brown dress. Grace turned back to the corpse, but found it to be gone.

"He was waiting for his lover when the guards caught him," the female voice said. Grace turned back to her and found the woman looking up into the tree as if she could see the limp body.

"What happened?" Grace found her voice to be small.

"He and his lover were set to meet here that night," the woman said as she moved around Grace, "They should not have been out, but they both felt their love could not bear the parting. The town guard was also out, but their reason more sinister. A highwayman had been pausing travellers along this way. One of his victims had tried to fight the highwayman for the gold in his pouch and the highwayman had left him barely alive in the road. As the man had been a member of the town council it was decided that something must be done about the highwayman

"The town guard came across the man as he waited here for his lover. He denied being the highwayman as they beat him. When he no longer could defend himself verbally they wrapped the rope snug around his throat and declared him judged fairly."

"And I suppose you are his lover haunting this place as vengeance," Grace said, surprised her own voice was so strong.

"Oh, she is here too," the woman tilted Grace's hand back up toward the tree. This time Grace could see the second body hanging from a nearby branch.

"She arrived as they were beating him," the woman said, "She tried to stop them and tell them that he was her lover. They did the only thing their minds claimed was right and she was sent away with him."

"Then who are you to them?" Grace asked.

"She was my sister," the woman answered, "I told her not to go. She didn't listen to me. It destroyed our mother. Hardly a ripple was felt in town and none of the guard bothered doing any more than burying them in unmarked graves."

"And the highwayman?" Grace asked.

"Never stopped a soul along this road," the woman

answered.

"Then perhaps the man was the highwayman," Grace said.

"That is what the guards thought," the woman said, "But no, it was the innocent who were murdered here."

"What do you want from me?" Grace asked, "There is nothing I can do for them."

"You are right," the woman said, "You can do nothing for them. I am the one asking the favour, I need you to deliver a message."

"To who?" Grace asked.

"A sailor who has just arrived at the port," the woman said, "His name is Jacob. Tell him what happened to Eaton and Audrey. Tell him that Hazel still loves him."

"I have to get home," Grace said.

"This errand shan't take you long," the woman said touching Grace's arm. Then she was gone. Grace shined the lantern all around, but the woman was no longer there. Grace checked the corpses and found them gone as well. Everything was back to the way it had been when Grace had started along this road.

Grace started forward again. She turned down the road leading back to the farm, but found herself going along the other road. This road went the opposite direction from the farm as it went to the ocean and the port there. Despite trying, Grace couldn't turn around or change her direction. With a sigh, she let the road take her forward.

With her feet tired and sore, Grace found herself standing on the docks of the port. It was still before midnight and dark. There were several ships in the port, but none on the wharf where Grace had arrived. She wondered if the woman had gotten something confused when she heard a sound from out in the ocean. There was a ship out there and it was coming towards shore.

In minutes the ship was docked at the wharf and the gangplank was coming down. Only one man came out of the ship and along the wharf towards her. Grace might as well have been the only person in the world for the amount of attention the man paid to his surroundings. He appeared as real as the woman in the forest.

"Are you the one?" the man asked, "Are you the one she sent?"

"I think so, if your name is Jacob," Grace said, "She said to tell that Eaton was mistaking for the highwayman and hung while Audrey was hung for trying to stop them."

"The guards found their scapegoat," Jacob said, "Innocent blood on their hands."

"The lovers were buried in unmarked graves," Grace said.

"It must have been hell on Hazel," Jacob said, "Her mother always preferred Audrey. It is no wonder she never joined me out here. There was no way she could get away from home."

"She said to tell you that Hazel still loves you," Grace said.

"It adds joy to my heart to hear that," Jacob said, "I never would have left had she not sent me away and I have waited much too long to hear news of her."

"She sent you away?" Grace asked, "Then she was supposed to meet her lover as well?"

"Hazel would never have met me there," Jacob said with a shake of his head, "We had met up in town when she could separate herself from her sister for a brief moment. She told me to leave and meet her at the port. I waited for her as long as I could, but then I had to take a job as a sailor. But if it safe to return to her than that is what I shall do."

Jacob went passed Grace and started walking. Grace turned around, but he was gone. Noises from along the wharf assaulted her as they had been there before. Also there were people in a group further down. Grace found herself able to move of her own free will.

It didn't take Grace long to find someone with a wagon willing to take her back to the farm. She counted herself lucky to have enough coinage to be able to pay them. The gentleman didn't talk along the way, which meant that Grace didn't have to answer any questions. When they reached the intersection of the three paths, Grace looked around. Nothing was different about it. It was the same as she had left it. She had hoped to at least see whether Jacob made it back to Hazel. The driver turned the direction of the farm.

Grace glanced back at the intersection over her shoulder. Two figures stood there in the moonlight. Both were young. One she recognized as Jacob. The other could only be Hazel with the way she greeted him. Grace turned back around. The gentleman dropped her off beside the gate rather than near the porch because there was more room to turn around. Grace walked the distance to the house. The windows were dark except the kitchen.

Grace went inside to the kitchen and found her grandmother seated the table with two cups and the tea pot.

"You missed supper," her grandmother said, "And your mother is upset at your absence but she had to go to bed." Her grandmother poured the two cups of tea.

"Well, where were you?" her grandmother asked.

Grace explained everything from the moment she got near the meeting of the three paths until she hired the man to drive her back to the farm. Her grandmother nodded as if she understood everything that happened.

"But how could she?" Grace asked when she had finished with her story.

"How could she what?" her grandmother asked.

"How could she send him away if she loved him?" Grace asked.

"How could she not?" her grandmother responded, "Hazel had heard the guards talking about what they were going to do and that is why she sent him away."

77

"I don't understand," Grace said.

"Jacob was the highwayman," her grandmother said, "Now off to bed with you."

The Best Brownie Recipe

B. Heather Mantler

MR. HAGUE'S DEATH

I sat in the chair across from Mr. Hague with the offered glass of scotch in my hand and stared him straight in the eyes. His grey eyes stared back.

"Are you sure you want me to do this?" I asked.

"Yes," Mr. Hague answered with firm conviction, "I would much rather it be done by a friend, who will do it properly than an enemy who would mess it up. I trust you."

"None of your family will when they find out," I replied.

"Maybe someday they will understand," Mr. Hague answered.

"Then you don't mind if I ask for the full fee up front," I said.

"I expect nothing less," Mr. Hague replied.

I took a sip of the scotch. My refinement suggested coughing it back up, but I had enough self-control to keep it down. Mr. Hague was kind enough to pretend he didn't notice. I placed the glass on the edge of the desk.

"How is Molly?" Mr. Hague asked. He always sounded like he genuinely wanted to know rather than trying to fill empty air.

"Quite well," I answered, "Every time I see her she

seems to be bigger and sweeter."

"Still can't get custody?" Mr. Hague asked.

"Her father's mother has been collecting evidence against me and fights to keep Molly every time we go to court," I answered, "And there seems to be a lot of awful stuff to be put out there."

"What about her father?" Mr. Hague asked.

"Hasn't been seen since Molly was six-months-old," I answered, "But he left no custody instructions."

"What does Molly say?" Mr. Hague asked.

"She keeps asking when she is coming home with me," I answered.

"I can help you if you would like," Mr. Hague said.

"Not if your family is going to dig it up and use it against me," I said.

"I'll think about a way to help," Mr. Hague said.

"You have limited time," I said.

"I very much understand that," Mr. Hague said.

There was a knock at the study door. It opened after he called for the person to come in. The butler stepped into the room.

"You called, sir," the butler said. It appeared almost as if he would have given a stiff bow but caught himself. He lacked the British accent, but still spoke with a certain stiffness.

"I need the usual contract and the full payment," Mr. Hague said.

"Are you sure, sir?" the butler asked.

"Yes," Mr. Hague answered.

"Very well," the butler said, "I will get them immediately." The butler left the study and closed the door on the way out.

"Unfortunately this is the last contract you will have from me," Mr. Hague said, "You will have to find another patron."

"I have other clients," I said, "They should tide me over

until then."

"Good," Mr. Hague said.

The door opened and the butler came back in. He closed the door before coming to the desk. The butler offered Mr. Hague the paper first. Mr. Hague carefully uncapped his pen. With care he fixed the cap on the other end of the pen. With precision, he wrote the necessary details on the lines applicable to the job. Only once he checked over and signed it, did he offer it to me. I checked the details he had filled in. It was exactly as he said. I signed on the appropriate line. I looked up at Mr. Hague. He nodded. I folded the contract and tucked it into my pocket.

"Pay Miss. Bennett," Mr. Hague told the butler. The butler nodded before taking out and handing me an envelope. His manner suggested he knew more about the contract I had just signed then he was supposed to. I gave no physical response and tried to keep it out of my eyes. He moved away once I had the envelope. I didn't check the amount before tucking it in beside the contract.

"Thank you," I said, "I will see you again in a few weeks."

"Of course," Mr. Hague said.

I got to my feet before following the butler out of the study. He led the way to the front door. We didn't meet any of the family along the way. The butler opened the front door for me. He followed me out and closed the door behind him.

"You can't do this," the butler said keeping his voice down. There was panic leaking across his face.

"Not only have I agreed to do it, but I've been paid," I said, "There is nothing either of us can do about it. At least let him have his dignity."

The butler fought his internal battle. I waited it out. Finally he settled on something he could live with for the moment. The butler nodded to me before going back inside.

My little bachelor apartment was echoy this evening as my loneliness was overpowering. I had money today thanks to Mr. Hague and his last contract, but I lacked the motivation to find the alcohol necessary to drown it all out. Instead I sat curled up on my mattress staring out my window at the view of the city. The sun was shining on the carious colours of roofs. As much as I could hear the traffic I couldn't see any of it.

I wished Molly could be here, but she was not allowed to stay with me. As her mother, I got supervised visits one afternoon a week, barring any scheduled conflicts. Back when I was younger and less experienced, I had promised Molly that she could come live with me. She remembered that promise and asked after every visit if this time she could go home with me. I had to bury my emotions as I explained not this week. Jared's mother would roll her eyes and make impatient noises during the whole exchange.

I wish that Jared was here. He would hold me close and tell me everything just looked bad in the moment. But then Molly would be with us. And we would be all living in the house. That two day job would no longer be the biggest regret of my life. He was supposed to be taking care of Molly, by instead his mother barred my way and cut me off from my daughter. She had said she had been left with custody when he had to leave town for work. Some days I suspect that when she found out he had a child she murdered him and hid his body away where it would never be found. But there was no proof of that.

The phone rang. Given that tomorrow was visiting day that could only mean one thing. I didn't reach for it. I didn't want to hear her voice and whatever made up excuse she had this time. My arms tightened around me as I squeezed my eyes shut. It didn't stop the ringing. No the ringing continued until the answering machine picked it up.

"Lucy," Jared's mother's voice came through the phone line, "Molly has an appointment and as such she cannot see you. Perhaps next week." The click spoke as much as the message. I was left with only the echo of what had been. If given the option she would not leave me with even that. I was not worthy of her granddaughter's time and attention. As far as the courts were concerned I had signed over custody to Jared and he had left Molly in his mother's custody. It was not Molly I signed to give him custody.

I laid my head down on the pillow. There was no reason to sleep. No reason to get tomorrow. Except that I was tired. I needed the rest. Yes, I was losing the war but that didn't mean I was going to give up the fight. And wishing was not going to do me any good.

Mr. Hague set his pen down with a sigh. He was physically tired. There had been a time not that long ago when he could work late into the night. Now he tired in late evening.

"Sir?" the butler asked from where he was standing in the doorway. This was his usual routine at ask Mr. Hague if he needed anything else for the night. My. Hague looked at the butler. Tonight the worry lines were prominent, as they had been since Lucy Bennett's visit. Mr. Hague had nothing to say that would sooth this trusted servant.

"Yes," Mr. Hague answered. The butler stepped into the study as he did when Mr. Hague said he needed something else.

"How do you find a man no one else has been able to locate?" Mr. Hague asked. The butler looked surprised at such a question.

"Why did he disappear?" the butler asked.

"I don't know," Mr. Hague answered, "From my understanding he left his daughter with his mother and said he would be back in a few days. No one has seen him since."

"Why did he leave?" the butler asked, "Was it for work? For leisure? Did he want to go? Was he forced to go?"

"Those are good questions," Mr. Hague said, "I will have to continue my quest tomorrow pondering those questions."

"If I may ask, who are you looking for?" the butler asked.

"Jared Collins," Mr. Hague answered, "I told Miss. Bennett, I would help her get custody of her child. After talking it over with my lawyer after finding out as much as I could about the situation, he suggested finding the father would likely get me farther than anything else."

"Could she not apply for custody through the courts?" the butler asked.

"She had tried numerous times but no judge has been willing to grant it," Mr. Hague answered, "Jared's mother had evidence suggesting that Miss. Bennett has a lifestyle which could be harmful to a child. This has led to supervised visits once a week and no other contact allowed. There is even claim that his mother has a piece of paper that Miss. Bennett signed granting Jared full custody of their child. Since Jared is missing and before he left he asked his mother to take their daughter, that gives his mother full custody."

"Where was Miss. Bennett while Mr. Collins was leaving town?" the butler asked.

"Re-entering the country," Mr. Hague answered, "She had been out of the country on business. I assumed that was why he asked his mother to babysit as Miss. Bennett had been living in the same house as he was before the trip. After the trip, she found herself an apartment."

"Then you definitely need to find Mr. Collins," the butler said, "He seems to be the only one who could straighten the whole situation out."

"That was my thoughts," Mr. Hague said, "But finding him seems to have several problems associated with it."

"Perhaps something to work on tomorrow," the butler said.

"Today you may be right," Mr. Hague said. He checked his desk before pushing his chair back. The butler covered his surprise as he followed Mr. Hague out of the study and closed the door after the light was turned off. Both men headed to their separate bedrooms for the night.

I slouched in the borrowed car as I stared over the dashboard. I wasn't supposed to be here but I couldn't help myself. I would be fine as long as I wasn't noticed. Fortunately there was plenty of other cars parked along the side of the road. Not all of them related to the school session that was about to end.

Jared's mother's car squeezed into a space on the other side of the road. She got out and joined the group of mothers standing near the entrance. They let her into the group as if she naturally fit there. She probably did. They wouldn't recognize me as Molly's mother because I wasn't allowed to pick her up from school.

The bell rang. More parents moved toward the school building but otherwise nothing changed. I stayed still and kept my breath shallow. If I was caught she would work to make sure I never saw Molly again and the judge would listen because I didn't play by the rules.

The children came pouring out. Some headed directly for their parents while others went for the playground. A few stayed among friends. Some parents called their children while others let their children come on their own. Jared's mother waited. I didn't see Molly among the first charge. As it cleared I realized it was because she hadn't been part of it. She came with reluctance and the world on her shoulders. There was no smile for her grandmother and her grandmother barely acknowledged her. Instead the woman continued her conversation with the other mothers. Molly found a spot to sit behind her grandmother to wait.

It would have been easy. I would need her attention, which wouldn't be difficult. Jared's mother would never notice. Then it was a matter of getting her into the car. She would come readily and no one would see it as different from every other parent in the line-up of cars. We could be out of the reach of the courts in hours.

I turned the engine on. After waiting for a clear space, I slipped the car into traffic. I drove passed the school and the unhappy little girl in need of her mother. At the first red light I sat up to see better.

I had places to go and things to do, especially since I had been paid. Instead I found myself driving to Jared's house. I parked out on the front curb. I got out and leaned against the passenger side door. The house looked the same. The outside was likely maintained by the same company as Jared originally hired. I crossed the arms over my chest.

Mrs. Kest came out of her house next door. She had her gardening gloves and trowel, but came over as soon as she saw me.

"How are you?" Mrs. Kest asked, "I haven't seen you in at least a year."

"I've been told I am not welcome here," I answered.

"But that is ridiculous," Mrs. Kest said, "Molly lives there. Parents should be with their children."

"Jared's mother doesn't think so," I replied.

"That bitch shouldn't be anywhere near Molly," Mrs. Kest said, "The amount of neglect I have witnessed from that woman."

"Would you be willing to testify to that?" I asked, "Because so far the court believes her to be a saint and I haven't found any evidence to prove otherwise."

"But there can't be much evidence to keep you away from Molly," Mrs. Kest said.

"Apparently I am an absent parent, neglectful, undeserving of a child, and I signed my custody rights away," I replied.

"None of those sound like you," Mrs. Kest said.

"But the evidence presented in court tell otherwise,"

"That is wrong," Mrs. Kest said, "I will see what I can do."

"Thank you," I said. Mrs. Kest headed off to work in her garden. She was starting work just as Jared's mother's car vehicle turned onto the street. The vehicle slowed as if the driver was not sure about continuing, but then it finished its journey to the driveway. She parked in front of the garage, likely because she couldn't get into the garage.

The back door of the vehicle flew open and Molly burst out. She came across the lawn at speed. I caught her when she leaped at me. The smile was huge and the world was no longer her burden to carry. She was just my happy and sweet little girl.

"Molly," Jared's mother called.

Her arms tightened around my neck as if she was worried I might let go

"You aren't supposed to be here," Jared's mother said.

"It is my day for visiting," I responded without letting go of Molly.

"I called you yesterday," Jared's mother said, "And I told you that it wasn't possible because Molly has an appointment."

"What kind of appointment?" I asked.

"You need to leave," Jared's mother said.

"You have no right to keep things from me about Molly," I said, "Even the court agreed on that."

"I don't want to go," Molly's voice was muffled by my jacket.

"It is nothing serious," Jared's mother said, "But you need to leave because we have to get her ready to go."

"No go," Molly said squeezing tighter.

"I think whatever this appointment is both important and necessary for me to know," I said, "If Molly doesn't want to go there is a good reason."

"Of course she doesn't want to go," Jared's mother said, "She thinks she'll get more attention if she makes a fuss."

"What is this appointment?" I asked.

"Just a doctor's appointment," Jared's mother answered, "You are both making a big deal out of nothing."

"If it was no big deal you would tell me why she needs a doctor's appointment," I said.

"I am not telling you because it isn't important," Jared's mother said, "If it were important I would be forced to tell you. Now you must go as we have to get ready to go. Molly, come on." The last sentence was on order. Molly squeezed tighter and shook her head into my shoulder.

"Why don't you want to go?" I kept my voice soft.

"Hurts," Molly answered, "Every time the doctor gives me a shot. I don't want anymore."

"Unfortunately, there is nothing I can do about it today," I said, "But I will do what I can to make sure you don't have to go again."

"You promise?" Molly asked.

"I promise," I answered, "Now you have to go with your grandmother, but I'm doing what I can to change things."

"Okay," her answer held all of her disappointment and I struggled to not just pack her into the car and away from her grandmother. She hugged me tighter before letting go. I gave her a half-smile, which she returned.

Jared's mother ushered Molly inside, but Molly gave me one last pleading look. The door closed and I stood there feeling empty. So many people in the world I wanted to curse, but it wouldn't do me any good. I went back and got into the car. I wasn't sure where to go, but I couldn't stay here. Probably should find something to eat. I turned the ignition and put the car into drive.

Mr. Hague looked up at the sound of knocking on his study door. It opened and the butler stepped inside.

"Your lawyer as you requested," the butler announced before the man stepped into the room. Mr. Hague stood up as his lawyer came towards the desk. His knees wanted to buckle, but he fought against any such weakness.

"How are you this afternoon?" the lawyer asked as they shook hands. The butler left the room as the lawyer sat down in the chair in front of the desk.

"I'm getting by," Mr. Hague answered.

"Still going through with your plan?" the lawyer asked.

"Contract is already out," Mr. Hague answered, "And plans are in place."

"That was fast," the lawyer said.

"I have a limited amount of time," Mr. Hague said.

"So, what do you need from me today?" the lawyer asked.

"The custody dispute I called out about yesterday," Mr. Hague answered, "Apparently the neighbour is willing to testify to the grandmother's neglect."

"Might help," the lawyer said, "But based on the records I received, it may not be enough."

"Miss. Bennett called me today," Mr. Hague said, "The grandmother has been taking the daughter lots of doctor appointments and refuses to tell Miss. Bennett the reason why. The grandmother claims the appointments are nothing important enough to talk about."

"That sounds like a serious problem," the lawyer said, "I suppose the appointments are not with the doctor listed in the file."

"Miss. Bennett called the doctor, who would be listed in the file, and his office didn't know anything about the appointments," Mr. Hague said.

"That is a problem," the lawyer said, "Miss. Bennett made sure the grandmother couldn't take the daughter to any other doctor without very good reason. As well as any changed in doctors has to be discussed and agreed upon by everyone involved. There has been no record of any changes in doctors. Did Miss. Bennett figure out the doctor's name?"

"She didn't," Mr. Hague answered, "And she doesn't

think she could figure it out without breaking into Jared's house and looking for the information."

"Doesn't she have a key?" the lawyer asked, "I know the grandmother refuses to let her inside, but she was living there at one point."

"I do not know," Mr. Hague said, "She used the words break in."

"Since the grandmother has taken possession of the house, stepping inside probably counts as breaking in," the lawyer said, "Did she say how often these appointments are happening?"

"Every two weeks or so," Mr. Hague answered, "Miss. Bennett said the grandmother schedules the appointments to conflict with her visits with her daughter. Since the appointment is during when Miss. Bennett is supposed to see her daughter, the supervised visits get cancelled."

"The grandmother is stretching the custody agreement," the lawyer said, "Miss. Bennett has full right to see her daughter whether her daughter has an appointment during the court arranged time. I think I need to talk to Miss. Bennett personally. The grandmother is no longer following the court rulings and may be placing the child in danger. I need her permission and signature to file with the court."

"How soon is the hearing likely to be?" Mr. Hague asked as he started sorting through the top layer of material on his desk.

"Hopefully this week," the lawyer answered, "But it may depend on which judge is available to hear the case. I will push for it to be heard as soon as possible. Have you gotten anywhere in the search for the father?"

"I have someone from his work place looking for files on him," Mr. Hague answered, "They are supposed to get back to me later today."

"They are willing to give up that information?" the lawyer asked.

"The supervisor I talked to didn't even recognize his name," Mr. Hague answered, "He was going to look through their files for any information they could give me. But he didn't promise me much beyond calling me back. He could call and say that he can't give me any information. I have a few other leads, but none of them have gotten back to me."

"Hopefully that is sorted out soon," the lawyer said, "His presence would remove the grandmother completely. Has Miss. Bennett explained about the custody agreement she signed?"

"No," Mr. Hague said as he took a paper from the bottom of the pile, "She hasn't said anything. Why?"

"The agreement doesn't mention their daughter by her name," the lawyer said, "If it was a legal custody agreement their daughter would be named as well as other information about their daughter. Instead the agreement just signs over custody of something that is unnamed for an indefinite period unless he does something reckless against whatever it was. But whatever they had the agreement about is unnamed."

"Well, you can ask her," Mr. Hague said, "I found her number." Mr. Hague started to dial.

I had just locked the door to my apartment when I heard the phone ring. I thought about going back in to try and catch it, but I had an appointment to keep. Since I only had half an hour from the first call to meeting the client. I might have been more worried, but it wasn't a new client and I already knew about his paranoia. Whoever was calling was just going to have to wait. I hope it wasn't too important. The particular client tended to send me places with limited time to prepare and this job didn't appear to be any different.

After seeing Molly and calling Mr. Hague, I had decided the best thing to do at the moment was to distract myself with work. It hadn't taken long to get a response. Since it was a client I had worked for in the past, I didn't have to worry about doing reference checks or any other checks. That made things easier. I probably should have told Mr. Hague about my plans to take on work, but things had settled so quickly and he was likely busy. I headed down the hall.

"She is not picking up," Mr. Hague said as he set the receiver back.

"Did she mention her plans for the day?" the lawyer asked.

"No," Mr. Hague answered, "But this situation with her daughter is bringing her down. When she is looking for a distraction, Miss. Bennett goes back to work."

"Then it may be days before we can talk to her or get her signature," the lawyer said.

"I can find a copy of her signature," Mr. Hague said.

"That poses several ethical problems for me," the lawyer said, "I know you don't see them but it could damage my career to do or even know about such fraud. No, I need her signature. I can do what I can and you will let me know once you can get a hold of her."

"She does have a place on the web that she can be contacted through," Mr. Hague said, "But I don't use it as I am never in that much of a hurry to contact her."

"And you don't care much for using the web," the lawyer said, "Give me the information on the website."

Mr. Hague opened the door to his right and went through a stack of cards. He removed one and offered it to the lawyer before putting the rest back. The lawyer looked it over before putting it in his pocket.

There was a knock on the study door. Mr. Hague called out for the person to come in. The door opened and his son stepped inside.

"I am sorry to disturb your meeting," his son said, "But

supper is ready."

"I should be going anyway," the lawyer said, "As I said I will go and do what I can." The lawyer got up out of the chair.

"Thank you," Mr. Hague said. He remained seated. The lawyer nodded before leaving the study.

"What was that about?" his son asked.

"I am trying to a favour for a friend," Mr. Hague answered, "And it is more complicated than I had first thought."

"You are paying your lawyer's fees for a favour?" his son asked.

"It is my money," Mr. Hague answered, "And I will spend it as I wish. Also it is never a waste of money if it is spent for a good cause."

His son shrugged and left the study. Mr. Hague sighed before moving his chair away from the desk. His knees weren't sure about getting up, but Mr. Hague was not going to let the break down on his body to prevent him from living. He got and went for supper.

I was sitting on the plane having been right about my current client and his want to get the job started immediately. He bought me the window seat on a non-busy night flight. I had no seat mates, though there was a couple in the seats in front of me. The stewardess had done her rounds, so I was left alone to my own thoughts.

I took out my tablet. It took a moment to connect to the nearest wifi before I could surf the internet. There was not much actually new on the news sites. Before I could move to some of the more questionable sources of news, a notice popped up in the corner. I tapped it and the message centre opened it.

It was a message from a Aaron Burroughs. I hesitated for a moment. The name seemed familiar, but I didn't know him. I tapped the message. Mr. Burroughs was Mr. Hague's lawyer and he was working on the case of getting me custody of Molly. He had gotten all the records from all the previous court hearings from the man I had used as a lawyer. The man wasn't a bad lawyer, but he hadn't been all that helpful. And apparently he was more than willing to turn the whole thing over to Mr. Burroughs without even my signature. Fortunately, if Mr. Burroughs worked for Mr. Hague he was likely more than compete.

Mr. Burroughs needed my signature to take the case before the court again. He also wanted to know what the custody agreement between me and Jared was really about and why the subject was not written on the document. The non-legal and very unofficial document that Jared had found on the internet, which had been making my life a living hell since his mother had found it in his office. On the other hand, she didn't have access to the garage.

I sent a message back to Mr. Burroughs that I would only be gone from the city for forty-eight hours and I would gladly meet with him when I got back. I even offered places and times. I had already taken down my posting about my availability so there were no more jobs waiting for me. That made for plenty of free time. The places were coffee shops and very public restaurants. I don't meet people in places where I cannot get away if I need to, whether they had good references or not. I had not checked with Mr. Hague as to Mr. Burroughs being his lawyer or not. That placed a level of dis-trust, but I can work with that because that was what I did for work.

I shut down my tablet. I didn't want to look at any more news sites. I just wanted to be distracted by something else. I tucked the tablet into my bag and removed the pill bottle. I took out a pill and put that back as well. Using the water supplied by the stewardess on her last round, I washed the sleeping pill down. Then I settled in to try and sleep.

Despite his physical exhaustion, Mr. Hague found

himself unable to sleep so he was now sitting in his study watching the sun wander across the back lawn. He had been sitting there since it had been dark and he had seen the sunlight since it has arrived. Mr. Hague thought he should get some work done, but his brain was fogged in from the tiredness.

The phone rang. Mr. Hague turned back to his desk and picked up the receiver. His hello got the caller to identify himself.

"This is David Grave of the Shuffler Company," the man said, "We talked yesterday."

"Yes," Mr. Hague said, "Did you find the file on Jared Collins?"

"I did," Mr. Grave answered, "According to the file he hasn't worked for the company in five and half years."

"Was he fired or did he quit?" Mr. Hague asked.

"It was a mutually agreed among parting," Mr. Grave answered.

"And what date was that?" Mr. Hague asked.

"July 6," Mr. Grave answered.

"What was he working on at the time?" Mr. Hague asked.

"I am sorry I can't tell you that," Mr. Grave said.

"I supposed you can't tell me what position he held either," Mr. Hague said.

"I can't," Mr. Grave said, "I have given you all the information I can."

"I have one more question," Mr. Hague said, "And then I'll leave you alone."

"All right," Mr. Grave said.

"Where was Jared Collins when this mutual parting happened?" Mr. Hague asked.

"I don't have that information," Mr. Grave said, "As I said there is very little information I can share and I have not much more available to me."

"Thank you for what you have given me," Mr. Hague

said, "I appreciate you taking the time to help me."

"You are welcome," Mr. Grave said. Mr. Grave hung up. Mr. Hague listened to the silence for a moment before putting down his end. He turned back to the window and let his mind process the information.

Jared Collins went off to work on July first and was not heard from again. Except the company had heard from him or knew what happened to him. Mr. Hague doubted that Mr. Collins had been part of the mutual decision to part ways with the company he worked for. He must have gotten himself in trouble and the company didn't want to be connected to it. All Mr. Hague had to do was figure out where he had been sent and how to get him back.

Mr. Hague turned back to his desk and picked up the phone. He dialed the number and waited. It was answered in short order.

"This is Mr. Hague. I need some information about Jared Collins. I need to know when he left the country and where he went. Thank you."

Mr. Hague hung up the phone. He sorted some of the papers on his desk as he waited. It was only fifteen minutes before the phone rang. Mr. Hague picked it up and listened for a moment.

"Is he still there?" "Thank you for the information." Mr. Hague hung up the phone. Once again he turned back to the window to ponder the information.

There was a knock at the door. Mr. Hague turned around as the butler entered the study.

"Your lawyer is back to see you," the butler said, "Would you like breakfast brought to you after your meeting?"

"Yes," Mr. Hague answered as the lawyer stepped inside. The butler nodded and then left. He closed the door behind him. The lawyer sat down in the chair and skipped the handshake today. Mr. Hague was grateful because he was not sure he could stand that long.

"I contacted Miss. Bennett and we set up a meeting at the coffee shop the day after she gets back," the lawyer said, "Though I had suggested she could drop by my office as soon as possible."

"She doesn't trust people to be who they say they are," Mr. Hague said, "The only way she would have agreed to drop by your office is if I had introduced you to her in person. It is a habit formed due to her choice in occupations."

"Well, we have a meeting scheduled," the lawyer said, "And I am working to have the hearing scheduled for the day after. Did Mr. Collins' work get back to you?"

"They did," Mr. Hague answered, "He was let go five days after he disappeared."

"Is he still alive?" the lawyer asked.

"I believe so," Mr. Hague answered, "No one has tried to contact his family to have his body returned. On the first of July he left his daughter with his mother and boarded a flight to Eastern Europe. He never returned and the company ended his employment with them on the sixth."

"Something happened during those five days," the lawyer said, "Have you spoken with our diplomat in that area?"

"Not yet," Mr. Hague answered, "It is still too early in the day. As much as I want to solve this, I don't wish to be a pester to people who have helped me in my life."

"What are you going to do about your family?" the lawyer asked, "They obviously don't know about your plan."

"I haven't been able to tell them," Mr. Hague answered, "The only one who even knows I'm sick is the butler. I have tried at various times throughout my son's life to teach him about my businesses, but he always turns away. When he was a child, I tried to be a father. I was there for his school and sports events. I would listen to him talk about his day. I would sit at his bedside in the evening and tell him stories until he went to sleep. I tried to teach him proper money management. Whenever he asked about his mother, I told him about her death during his birth. I told him how much she had wanted a child and that he was her miracle. I worked hard to be the father she would want me to be.

"But he never reached out. He never tried to connect. The more I tried to reach him the further he withdrew. He refused to listen when I talked about my businesses, or what I did with my day, or how I got the money he kept spending. As a child, he accepted his allowance and obeyed my rules about money. As a teenager, he demanded money for everything. If I refused him, he would steal it or make sure I had to pay for whatever he wanted some other way. When he came of age, I gave him a bank account to help him start off his life.

"He skipped going to the college he had been accepted into and instead disappeared with a group of friends. I couldn't even follow him because he withdrew as much money as he could at a time, all from the same bank. He refused to talk to me and I let him go do his own thing because children need the space to find themselves and their place in the world. In two years he had drained the bank account and was out of money. The bank called me to tell me and I told the man on the other end that it was none of my business. If he wanted more money he would have to put it back in.

"The bank managed must have repeated that message to him, which was a bad idea because somewhere along in his life he had become that spoiled rich kid who thought the world owned him everything. He trashed the office and left the bank manager cowering in the corner. The police arrested him. Everyone looked at me to save him from the fate he had made himself. I went to talk to him while he was in lockup. I told him that I was disappointed in him. I told him that men make their own destiny. I told him that he brought this misfortune on himself. He cursed me. If there had not been a barrier between us, he would have killed me right there. He went to prison and I did nothing to help him.

"While he was gone, my sister called me in need of help. Her ex-husband decided that adding physical abuse to the mental abuse he had been doing for years was fun. I gave her and her children rooms in my house. My nephew, Gabriel, was already interested in business and was everything I had hoped my son would be. It was as natural as breathing to start teaching him about my businesses. He absorbed it all and was soon taking college courses to help him get the credentials everyone wants these days. I didn't tell him about all of it. I didn't tell him about the questionable deals, the quasi-legal transactions, and the jobs I contracted Miss. Bennett to do. He is an honest businessman with a willingness to help out his fellow man.

"It was six months after he got out of prison when Connor showed up at the door. In all outward appearances he was a changed man. As much as I wanted to believe, as everyone else did, I saw in his eyes that he was same person who cursed me for not bending to his will. He came to ask for a loan as he was a bad risk and no one else was willing to fund him. He had an idea for a business."

"The one he currently runs?" the lawyer asked, "The one that helps out former convicts who no one will hire despite the fact that they are going straight?"

"That is the one," Mr. Hague said, "Gabriel drew up the loan agreement. Connor signed it. The money was handed over."

"But you destroyed the loan agreement," the lawyer said.

"I saw the good in what he was doing," Mr. Hague said, "Despite some of the questionable things he was doing with his share of the earnings; Connor was running an honest business. I wanted to reward him for doing a good thing.

He has done nothing since his release from prison which would suggest the experience didn't change him."

"But you believe he is the same person," the lawyer said.

"I don't know anymore," Mr. Hague said, "I thought I knew how to read people, but he has done nothing to make me suspicious. He moved in after I collapsed at my sister's funeral, because everyone thought I was in need of the care. But I surprised them all by being healthy."

"But you are not healthy," the lawyer said, "You haven't been since before that incident."

"They don't know that," Mr. Hague said, "And they are both so busy with their lives and businesses to bother with my day-to-day life."

"But they are going to make a fuss when it comes out what you planned," the lawyer said, "And everything you have done to help Miss. Bennett might be not."

"She said as much when I first offered," Mr. Hague said, "I thought maybe I could keep things quiet, but I have needed too much help. Now I am not sure what to do about it."

"I will do what I can through the court system for Miss. Bennett," the lawyer said, "And if you find Jared Collins, I very much doubt your family can do anything about Miss. Bennett. I question your will with what you have just told me."

"Why would I leave most of my fortune to my son?" Mr. Hague said, "Why wouldn't I leave more to my nephew? Because all they are getting is the businesses, which they will have to run to gain more money. My bank accounts will slowly be drained over the next week. By the time the contract is set for, I will be broke from giving all my friends things they need."

"That does make sense," the lawyer said, "As long as you are sure about this."

"I am very sure about this," Mr. Hague said, "Out of

every thing in my life, this is the one thing I am most sure of."

"Then I will continue my help for Miss. Bennett and leave you to find Jared Collins," the lawyer said.

"Thank you," Mr. Hague said as the lawyer got to his feet.

"Just know that I am not as sure about this as you are," the lawyer said. Mr. Hague nodded. As the lawyer left, the butler brought in breakfast.

Mr. Hague put the phone back in its place. He smiled to himself. It was the first time in weeks he felt satisfied with something he had done. Despite the solution not being his favourite. He disliked solving problems by throwing money at them as he felt it was the easy way out. But he was much too sick to fight this problem any other way. Bribe money, bail money, a plane ticket, and a cab ride were the end of this issue. Overall a good morning.

There was a knock on the door. Mr. Hague called for the person to come in. The door opened and his nephew stepped inside. Something was wrong, Mr. Hague could see that. Usually his nephew was happy, especially since the announcement of his wife being pregnant with their second child a few months ago.

"Yes?" Mr. Hague asked.

"There is a doctor outside looking for you," Gabriel said.

"Why?" Mr. Hague asked.

"He said that he was the doctor who helped you when you collapsed at my mother's funeral," Gabriel said, "He says he is worried about your health because he has not heard from you since then."

"Send him away," Mr. Hague said.

"Uncle," Gabriel said, "Is there anything wrong?"

"Of course not," Mr. Hague said, "I haven't bothered with the doctor because there is no reason to see him again."

"You have been spending a lot of time in here in your study," Gabriel said.

"Everything is fine," Mr. Hague said, "Just send the doctor away."

"I will," Gabriel said. He hesitated but then left the study.

My flight home had been more crowded than my flight out, but it had been a daylight flight. As soon as I have gotten through the tedious parts of the airport, I caught a cab into town. It dropped me outside the coffee shop. I had called Mr. Hague and he had confirmed Mr. Burroughs was his lawyer.

The coffee shop was one of those environmentally friendly places that offered organic coffee, dairy free cream, and non-sugar sweeteners. Most of the clients could easily be mistaken as being homeless, except that clothing was thrift store rather than trash bin. Mr. Burroughs stood out in his business suit and briefcase. He sat at one of the tall tables, but I doubted the recyclable cup in front of him contained coffee. By the way he was nervously playing with it, the cup was empty.

I slid into the chair opposite from him.

"I am Lucy Bennett," I said.

"Arron Burroughs," he said.

"Sorry for the meeting place but I find it safest to meet people I don't know in public spaces," I said.

"I understand," Mr. Burroughs said, "All I need is your signature." He took out a paper-clipped stack of papers from his briefcase and placed them on the table in front of me. I skimmed them before signing on the required lines.

"I also have a question," Mr. Burroughs said as he put the stack away.

"Go ahead and ask," I said.

"What was the custody agreement you signed about?"

Mr. Burroughs asked.

"The custody agreement is about the Speedster," I answered, "That was how Jared and I met. He was looking to buy a Vauxhall VX220 Turbo Opel Speedster and I was the closest person who owned one. It had been a gift from one of my clients so I had no interest in selling it. However, we ended up dating, which started into a serious relationship. Jared had claimed he had looked up other people who owned the same car, but if he actually did he never contacted them. When I got pregnant, he suggested we move into his house. We joked about the car. He offered to buy it again, but I refused. So he found a custody agreement online and as a joke I signed it as he had fun custody of the car. He didn't fill in the rest of the agreement because no one else was going to see it."

"Unfortunately, his mother found it and made assumptions," Mr. Burroughs said, "But that seems like something she would claim he left to her and sell it."

"It is stashed in the garage," I said, "And she can't get in there because Jared didn't leave her with a key."

"I'm surprised she didn't hire someone to open it for her," Mr. Burroughs said.

"She hasn't had him declared dead yet either," I said, "But I am sure they are in the plans somewhere."

"I will get these papers filed," Mr. Burroughs said, "And then I will let you know when the hearing will be."

"Okay," I said, "Thank you for this."

"It is something that needs doing," Mr. Burroughs said. He got up and left the coffee shop.

Mr. Hague stayed in his seat until the car stopped. Then he did not wait for the chauffeur to come around and open the door for him. Lately he would have waited in the car as to conserve energy, but today he stepped out on to the tarmac. The plane had stopped only moments before the car had. Mr. Hague leaned on the car as he waited for the door of the plane to open.

Minutes passed. The stairs were brought over and the door was opened. An official exited the plane and headed into the airport without even a glance at Mr. Hague. Next came the person Mr. Hague was there to see, or he assumed it was. The man glanced around before focusing on Mr. Hague. He came down the stairs. He was much too skinny with hair suggesting a long time between good hygiene habits. But five years forgotten in a cell of a prison that barely fed its occupants will do that. Fortunately someone had managed to get the man a bath.

"You must be the man I have to thank for me freedom," Jared Collins said to Mr. Hague before offering his hand.

"Well, part of that is correct," Mr. Hague said as he shook Mr. Collins hand. "I was inspired due to my promise to help a friend."

"I'm just grateful to be free," Mr. Collins said.

"There is a specific reason I got you out," Mr. Hague said.

"Perhaps you can tell me inside the car," Mr. Collins said, "You look tired."

"I am," Mr. Hague said. He opened the door and got inside. He slid over so Mr. Collins could get in as well. Mr. Collins closed the door once he was inside.

"This friend of yours," Mr. Collins said, "It would not be Lucy Bennet, would it?"

"It would," Mr. Hague said.

"I would have thought having a child would mean she could get into less trouble," Mr. Collins said.

"Her daughter is precisely the trouble," Mr. Hague said.

"Perhaps you should explain," Mr. Collins said. His expression was much more serious this time.

"Miss. Bennett returned from her job to find you had left and your mother in the house instead," Mr. Hague said.

"That was expected," Mr. Collins said, "As that was how I left things because I couldn't find her friend who we usually asked to babysit."

"Well, your mother refused Miss. Bennett entry to the house," Mr. Hague said.

"What!" Mr. Collins said.

"Instead she claimed she had been given custody," Mr. Hague said, "And when Miss. Bennett tried to take the matter to court, your mother brought out a document which showed that Miss. Bennet had signed away her right to custody."

"That document is not legally binding," Mr. Collins said, "It does not say Lucy gave up custody of Molly," Mr. Collins said, "Molly is not mentioned anywhere on it. The judge should have seen that."

"The judge agreed with your mother," Mr. Hague said, "Miss. Bennett was given once a week supervised visits."

"Why did you agree to help Lucy?" Mr. Collins asked.

"Because she accepted a contract very few others would have," Mr. Hague answered, "And I owe her for that."

"I need to go home then," Mr. Collins said.

"We will drop you off there," Mr. Hague said. He tapped the barrier and the chauffeur started the car.

"What does she think you are doing to help?" Mr. Collins asked.

"My lawyer has been working on going through the court system to sort out custody that way," Mr. Hague answered, "They were supposed to be at a hearing today, but it got cancelled until next week."

"Then we need sort things out in a hurry," Mr. Collins said, "Make things cheaper for the legal system. Though I suppose Molly won't recognize me."

Mr. Hague looked at Mr. Collins, but he had turned to stare out the window. He no longer noticed Mr. Hague's presence in the car. Mr. Hague left the man to his own thoughts.

"I hope she hasn't messed with the speedster," Mr. Collins muttered.

I stood on the doorstep of Mr. Hague's house. There were several vehicles in the driveway as if someone had guests. The butler must have been standing by the door as he opened it for me almost immediately after I had knocked. He looked at me. I could tell he didn't want to let me in. Finally he nodded and stepped aside. I entered and he closed the door before leading the way to the study.

The study was empty when we arrived.

"Mr. Hague is in his room," the butler said, "I will let him know you are here."

"Thank you," I said.

The butler turned away to leave the room.

"And I am sorry," I said.

The butler stopped. His head dipped, but he did not speak. He had accepted and was in mourning. He left and closed the door behind him.

I went to the side board. I poured two glasses of scotch. To one I added the contents of the vial from my pocket. I mixed it gently before putting the glass on the desk. I took the untampered with glass and sat down in the chair in front of the desk.

If there was anywhere in the world I could be today, I would not have picked here. The only thing holding me here was the contract and I had already received the payment in full. His lawyer had promised to keep working on the custody of Molly since the hearing had been cancelled for the second time. He promised a resolution as soon as possible. Rather than distract myself with work, I have sat waiting for messages from him. So far, I hadn't heard from him since he told me about the hearing being cancelled. He said he would let me know when the hearing would be rescheduled.

Tomorrow would be my next scheduled visit with Molly. We were going to spend the afternoon at the park. It was going to be a good day. After today I was going to need a good day.

The door to the study opened and Mr. Hague stepped inside. He closed the door before coming to sit in the desk chair.

"I took the liberty of pouring you a drink," I said.

"Thank you," Mr. Hague said. His hand hovered near the glass before setting his hand down on the cleaned off blotter.

"I did everything I could to help you with getting your daughter back," Mr. Hague said.

"I know," I said, "And I appreciate everything you have done."

Mr. Hague nodded, but he didn't try to add anything more. He picked up the glass and took a drink.

"Most people would be asking whether it will be painful or cause difficulties," I said.

"I trust you," Mr. Hague said. He finished the scotch. The lines on his face smoothed as if the world was easier to carry for right now.

"The pain is going away." Mr. Hague's voice was almost a whisper with plenty of awe. He got to his feet. He swayed slightly, but managed to get to the couch. He lay down and his eyes drifted closed.

The study door opened. I glanced away from Mr. Hague for a moment to see his son, Connor, standing in the doorway.

"What is going on?" Connor said coming into the couch, where his father was lying. He checked Mr. Hague's pulse.

"I am still alive," Mr. Hague's voice was drifting.

"What did you do?" Connor turned to me. His eyes danced with anger.

"Nothing I wasn't paid to do," I replied.

"Leave her alone," Mr. Hague said, "She has given me the one thing I wished for since my sister's funeral."

"What do you mean?" Connor asked turning back to his father.

"She has taken away my pain," Mr. Hague answered, "I only had another month likely anyway."

"Why didn't you say anything?" Connor asked, "What about treatment options?"

"It was terminal before I collapsed," Mr. Hague said, "It has spread to all the important organs. Treatments were useless. Money can't buy ev..."

Mr. Hague chest only rose a couple more times before he was still.

"How could you?" Connor turned back to me.

"Because he asked for that such mercy," I said as I got to my feet.

"Where are you going?" Connor asked.

"I am no longer under your father's employment," I said, "And I doubt I have any welcome left. You on the other hand have lots to do."

"You will be arrested for his murder," Connor said.

"Only if you can prove it is murder," I replied. Then I left. I passed the butler on my way out. He hurried toward the study rather than escort me out. My job was done and my contract fulfilled.

I was distracted as I pulled the borrowed car behind a car that looked like an Opel Speedster. It had been a long night and I hadn't gotten much sleep, but nothing was going to stop me from seeing Molly. I closed the door to the car and turned toward the park. Molly was up in the monkey bars while there was a man sitting on the bench facing away from me.

My mind wondered where Jared's mother was as I went toward the park. She was always somewhere she could watch and tsk to herself. Before I could think about things more, Molly saw me.

"Mommy," she cried. She swung down and landed with a crunch of gravel. She ran towards me and I opened my arms to embrace her.

"Mommy," Molly said, "Daddy's back."

"What?" I looked down at Molly.

"Daddy's back," Molly said. She extracted her arm and point to the man. He was no longer sitting facing the playground, but looking at us. I fell the rest of the way to my knees. He had aged badly over the last five years, but it was definitely Jared.

"Mommy," Molly said, "You're crying."

"I am," I said.

"But you should be happy," Molly said, "Daddy is back."

"I am happy," I said.

Jared had come over. He offered me a hand up. I took it. He was real. He was here. He pulled me into his arms. Molly's arms wrapped around one of my legs. Jared let go with one arm so he could pick up Molly and include her in the hug. I never wanted to let go.

B. Heather Mantler

A CLUSTER OF FRIENDS

I don't want to say that I was bored with my life, because if I did, I would owe Nicole two hundred dollars. Five years ago I swore I would never be bored with a normal life and a nine to five job. Now even my relationship has settled into a routine to the point where I know what time during the day he is going to text me. He isn't boring, but the routine is. I like routines, and usual am happy to settle into them, but sometimes I like shaking things up, which hadn't happened in four years.

My routine was to have lunch at my favourite café with James joining me and being seated at my favourite table. And today everything was the same with James joining me as I left the office. But as we got closer to the café I noticed someone was sitting at my table and a first I was okay with sitting at a different table, but then I realized it was Nicole. And now that I had seen her, I noticed her motorcycle parked at the curb. Anxiety and panic shot through me.

"You know maybe for today we could eat somewhere else," I suggested as I took James' arm.

"Just because someone else is at our table doesn't mean we need to go somewhere else," James replied shooing me into the café. The hostess smiled as she greeted us, but her eyes knew that my table was taken.

"You can seat us at the usual table," I told her. James was about to protest, but the hostess just took the menus into her arm and hurried to seat us. Apparently Nicole had warned her and she just needed me to confirm it.

Nicole looked smug as we came over. Before the hostess could seat us, I spoke up.

"James, this is my old 'friend' Nicole," I said, "Nicole, this is my boyfriend, James."

"Hello," Nicole said.

"Nice to meet you," James said. Only then did I let us sit down and accept the menus. I already knew what I was going to order, so I did not bother with the menu and instead focused on Nicole.

"What are you doing in town?" I asked as if I didn't know that she was out to stalk me and make me pay up the two hundred dollars.

"I'm on my way through to go see Jeremy," Nicole answered, "He is currently in hospice with terminal cancer."

"I can't image Jeremy like that," I said. The feeling of shock went through my system. Jeremy was the same age I was and I hadn't hit the middle ages yet. I would have thought this was one of Nicole's stories to get me back on the road, but sadness had flashed through her eyes when she spoke.

"But that is how things are," Nicole said, "How's your life here?" There was a sense of smugness back in her face and voice. She knew I owed her money, but I wasn't going to give in just yet. So, I started telling her about all the exciting things at work. James was nodding along as if this was all exciting, but Nicole had a serious face with laughter just about spilling out of her eyes.

The lunch was a little uncomfortable, but I got through it. James didn't seem at all fazed by it, but his eyes wondered a little as to the past I wouldn't talk about, which was where Nicole was from. I went back to work and my comfortable (if boring) space.

At supper, James suggested I go with Nicole to see Jeremy. He thought I needed it from the way I was reacting to things. I said I would think about.

After supper, I called Nicole and asked her where she was staying. She said she'd find a place. Remembering all the spaces she had stayed in the past, I offered her the couch. She accepted. After I hung up, James asked why I offered to let her stay at the apartment when she obviously made me uncomfortable. I shrugged and said she needed a place to stay.

Nicole arrived an hour later. By then I had pillows and blankets set out on the couch. She seemed tired so James and I retired to our room.

I found myself staring at the clock, which changed seconds at every glance. At midnight, I gave up. I slipped out of bed, being careful not to wake James. And I went out to the living room, where Nicole was lying on her side on the couch. She was awake and glanced up at me in the room lit by street lights as I sat down across the coffee table from her. I offered up the two hundred dollars I had taken off the nightstand as I had left the bedroom. She accepted it before sitting up and putting it away. She took a bottle of moonshine out of her bag. She offered and I took a sip before handing it back. We passed it back and forth a couple times before either of us spoke.

"Maybe you need to add some excitement to your life," Nicole said.

"How would you suggest?" I asked. My brain had been devoid of all ideas on the subject since I figured that to be the issue.

"You could add children to the relationship," Nicole

suggested.

"I don't think I can," I replied, "I had something as a teenager, which can cause such issues."

"That doesn't mean it has caused them," Nicole said.

"I've been off the pill for several months now," I replied before taking another sip of the alcohol.

"Maybe I should have asked for a pregnancy test before I shared my liquor," Nicole said taking the bottle back.

"Doesn't matter," I replied, "My period showed up two days ago."

Nicole mulled that over a moment before handing the bottle back.

"How's Jeremy the last time you heard anything?" I asked.

"The doctor is giving him less and less time to live every time he visits," Nicole answered, "Angela owns the hospice place, so he is getting good care."

"She was always good at that," I nodded. Nicole nodded in response but didn't say anything. I took a minute to really study her. I hadn't bothered at the café because she was just a tack in my personal bubble. Now I did so as an old friend who wasn't worried about an old bet.

Nicole was skinnier than the last time I had seen her, but she was always going without remembering to eat. This time, however, her cheeks were a little more hollow and her colouring was off in an unhealthy way. There were more sadness lines around her eyes and mouth, which hid when the focus was the smugness that came out. Her eyes held five long years of experiences that weren't all fun rides along the highway.

"How are you?" the question came out as a concerned friend before I could stop it. She had never liked such things as concerned friends before, but this time, she just sat back and looked tired. It was the tiredness which ached for sleep and rest but knew the only time those would come was when everything was final.

"Six months after you left, everyone else seemed to find their calling," Nicole answered, "And Cole got himself killed by playing chicken with a semi-truck. The poor driver ended up on the psych ward due to it all, despite everyone saying that the biker was the stupid one and he couldn't have stopped it. I gave his family the insurance money I was given by Cole's estate, after all the funeral expenses were paid. They needed it more than I did and they deserved it far more than any of Cole's family.

"Then a month later I crashed into a concrete barrier going a little too fast around a corner. My bike needed minor repairs and I was taken to the hospital with a broken leg. The doctor who fixed it up asked me out after transferring my care to a different doctor. I took him up on it. We clicked immediately and I was moved in by the end of the week. Two years later he dropped dead from cancer he didn't even know was in him. One of those ones where there are no symptoms and can kill with speed. I've been trying to figure out what to do with myself ever since. I've got a house and a car, but the highway sings in my blood.

"Anyway, Angela called a couple weeks ago and asked if I could come see Jeremy. She was going to try everyone, but I guess she didn't have your number. You coming?"

"I'm not sure I have much choice, except to go," I replied. Sure, there was a choice, but I was never much on turning away from a friend in actual need.

"I'm ready to go whenever you are," Nicole said as she put the cap back on the moonshine.

"Tomorrow," I replied as I got to my feet.

"Sure," Nicole replied. She lay back down, but she didn't look like she was going to get any sleep.

I climbed back into bed with James, but the clock informed me of every five-minute interval between the time I went back to bed and six in the morning.

A couple glasses of water and I followed Nicole in my car on our way to see Jeremy.

Nicole stopped semi-regularly at rest stops. I thought it was so that I could catch up because I would see her, drive passed, and she would catch up to pass me until the next rest stop. When we reached the hospice, Nicole was pale and shaky. She took a few minutes to sit on the steps and rest as well as take some sort of medication.

There appeared to be several things she didn't tell me about. One of which might be that it wouldn't be long before she needed a room in this same place.

Jeremy was lying in a small room with tubes coming from places no healthy person needed tubes. If those didn't make it hard to recognize him, then the fact that he was half the weight he was the last time I had seen him. Last time he was muscular and robust and, this time, he was skin and bones. The eyes were the same, though without as much laughter. There was no doubt he was dying.

Angela told me that Nicole and I were the first ones to make it out. I was sitting on the chair in the hallway outside Jeremy's room and she had sat down next to me. Her hand on my back was the only thing that felt real at that moment. The nausea just made everything more dream-like.

Angela went on to say that Jeremy was fighting in the hope the others would come. She was sorry she had not been able to reach me herself and that Nicole had to give me the news, but as owner and director of the hospice, her schedule only allowed her a certain amount of time. She offered me a tissue. Only then did I realize I was crying.

I ended up sleeping in my car because I wasn't really going to stay, so I didn't need to find a room somewhere. I'm not sure where Nicole stayed because her bike never moved from the parking stall. The others never showed up. Angela would tell us why, but I don't remember any of the excuses. It wasn't necessary to remember them. Brad showed up, though he was the one I never wanted to see again, and hadn't really been part of the group. Angela hadn't called him, someone else from the group had mentioned it and he decided to come and say goodbye because he and Jeremy had gotten along so well. He took a room at the nearby hotel. It was a nice room considering the age of the hotel.

Angela sat with me for a little while as I sat outside Jeremy's room. I tried to sit inside occasionally but always found myself back outside. Nicole sat there beside his bed for the afternoons. She looked like she needed the rest. One afternoon I heard them talking about what happens after death. It was like two people with a connection to the same subject that they understood each other on so many philosophical levels no one else could come close to understanding what they were saying. It chilled me and made me want to run. But I sat there and cried instead. There was nowhere to run anyway.

The death watch lasted another week. Not that Jeremy died at the end of that week. No, Nicole collapsed in the middle of a hallway after having a coughing fit where she was coughing up blood. A doctor was visiting one of the patients at the time and was able to examine her. He figured it was stage three or four lung cancer, especially after seeing the bottle of the pills she had been taking. I don't know if it was true, but she didn't wake up and Angela placed her in the room next to Jeremy.

Jeremy mustered all his strength to demand Angela phone Nicole's house and arranged for Nicole's three-and-a-half-year-old daughter to come say goodbye. Angela stopped in her duties as director instantly and made the phone call. When the person who was taking care of the girl made plans to come, Nicole was taken to the hospital for tests. It was all with the idea of finding some sort of treatment for her. Angela told me her doctor from home sent her records. Nicole had known about the cancer for six months and the trip had probably cost her energy she could have used to fight it.

I don't know why, but I looked up the records for Cole. His death was in the time frame Nicole had told me and he had been hit by a semi-truck. The driver did have issues from the incident. But the coroner had determined Cole had been playing chicken with the truck because the brain tumor was pressing against the parts of his brain which helped with impulse control. He would have been dead within two months anyway.

This led to a search of cancer rates from the small area of land we had called our hometown. It was part of a spike in that general piece of the country. It was above the national rate for cancers to the point of worrying scientists. Well, they had two more statistics of one kind, soon to become another kind. Angela looked over my shoulder and suggested regular checkups.

Nicole's daughter, Hailey, arrived the next day with her father's sister. Hailey's aunt was a rundown, older woman, who was had some negativity issues about losing work time and having a child dumped on her. Hailey herself was a bright, curious child, who had her mother's laughing eyes and a grin so infectious the sour-face secretary couldn't help but smile for the rest of the day. Hailey's smile all but went out at the sight of her mother lying in that bed. The three-year-old climbed up to be beside her mother. To hug her and talk to her. Nicole never responded and I don't know if she wanted to or not. I imagine that if she could've Nicole would have held her daughter and told her everything was going to be alright in the end, even if it didn't feel like it now. But I don't know that for sure.

I guess close friends are there til the end. Nicole and Jeremy left together, leaving their cancer rotten bodies behind. The friends I had thought were close never arrived for Jeremy's pain and still couldn't make it for the loss of the other. Angela's professionalism slipped as she fought her own emotional turmoil. I sat in the hallway with a three-and-a-half-year-old sitting on my lap. My own tears threatening to choke every time I tried to speak and her questions about what the people were doing with her mommy.

That night I lay on the back seat of my car and cried myself numb. I had tried to call James and talk but I found myself unable to say anything to him. He had never lost anything in his life, was there any way he could understand the loss of the past I never even acknowledged to him had it existed?

Jeremy's estate (if it could be called that) was settled quickly because everything had been sold to pay for his stay in hospice and all that money had been used up. There was only enough left to bury him. Since it was going to be a joint funeral with Nicole for the convenience of those who schedules prevented them from coming while they were alive, it wasn't going to cost too much.

Nicole's estate was a little more complicated. Her house had been sold already and the money put into a trust for Hailey. She was paying a monthly rent, which came out of the money her husband had left her when he had died. That money was to be used to take care of Hailey until she was old enough to be given access to the trust fund. Hailey's aunt was not mentioned in the will. The lawyer told me that both Nicole and her husband did not want her to be given full custody of Hailey because they felt the negativity would cause lasting damage to Hailey's mental wellbeing. Nicole left a note stating she only trusted a close friend with the custody of her daughter.

I suppose I should have called James and warned him before I arrived home with Hailey in tow, but it hadn't entered my mind. I had always thought that our relationship was good for the moment but really didn't need to last. He proved me wrong by not only accepting that I had left to say goodbye to an old friend and brought home a child but accepted that Hailey was now part of my family. He was already looking at listings for two room apartments before I had Hailey settled on the couch.

The Thursday after returning, I went in for a doctor's appointment. I asked him to run tests for all cancers I could have develop within my body. He had them all set up for the next week and an appointment scheduled for Monday to discuss the results.

James still hadn't found us a new apartment, but I guess I have to give him the new requirements. Because I am cancer free, but in the testing they found instead that I am a month into my pregnancy. I guess Nicole was right and I shouldn't have had any of the moonshine. Also, periods don't necessarily go away with pregnancy.

Next year I will do the same as Angela and go back from another round of tests. I need to do a favour for a friend and be around to watch her child grow up.

The Best Brownie Recipe

NOTES

This short story, Erin Blake, is a prequel for a novel I have not finished writing but do plan on getting done someday. I did not know there was a novel connected to it until after I finished writing the short story.

ERIN BLAKE

Mrs. Lisa Barton pulled up to the curb in front of the elementary school. Her black Mercedes stopping just before she put it in park. Mrs. Barton looked out the passenger side window for her granddaughter. The school yard had only a few children left waiting on parents and one teacher. Mrs. Barton did not see Madison. She shut off the car and got out.

"Madison," Mrs. Barton yelled. The children ignored her, but the teacher walked over.

"Madison was picked up just after school was let out, Mrs. Barton," the teacher said.

"By who?" Mrs. Barton asked.

"I didn't see," the teacher answered. Mrs. Barton reached into her car and grabbed her cell phone out of her purse. She flipped it open and dialed a number.

"Maria is Madison there?" Mrs. Barton asked, she paused for an answer, "Did Dennis phone to say he was going to pick her up?" After a pause she snapped the cellphone shut.

"Maria said that no one had picked up Madison," Mrs. Barton turned back to the teacher.

"She was over by the vehicles then she was gone," the teacher said, "I assumed she had been picked up."

Mrs. Barton opened her phone again and dialed a different number.

"Officer Schmitt," Mrs. Barton said, "Madison is missing."

Dennis Barton was sitting across the study from his father when his mother entered followed by Officer Schmitt.

"Is there something wrong?" Mr. Barton asked standing up. Mrs. Barton sank into a chair near the desk.

"Madison is missing," Mrs. Barton answered.

"What happened?" Dennis asked.

"We are here to try and figure that out," Officer Schmitt said. Mr. Barton sat back down.

"Mrs. Barton, why don't you start?" Officer Schmitt said.

"I went to pick up Madison," Mrs. Barton said, "But the teacher said someone else had already picked her up. The teacher didn't see who and none of the parents who were parked there saw anything."

"And Madison is?" Officer Schmitt asked.

"My granddaughter," Mrs. Barton answered.

"My daughter," Dennis said.

"And her mother is?" Officer Schmitt asked.

"Not in the picture," Dennis answered, "And hasn't been all her life. She wouldn't recognize Madison."

"And you don't think she would try to take Madison back?" Officer Schmitt asked.

"She would not," Dennis said. Officer Schmitt looked at Mrs. Barton, but she just shrugged.

"Is there anyone else you can think of who would take Madison?" Officer Schmitt asked, "Anyone who has made threats against your family?"

All three thought for several minutes.

Dennis pulled his car to the curb and turned off the engine. The house was middle class and well taken care of. There was no car in the driveway, but double garage could have held at least one.

"Is this the place?" Christine Patrick asked peering past Dennis to look at the house. Her lip was curling in disgust that she was trying to hide. As the girlfriend picked out by his parents, Dennis knew Christine was not used to associating with anyone who didn't live in a mansion.

"Yeah, this is it," Dennis said.

"And you think she might know where to find Madison?" Christine asked.

"No," Dennis answered, "But she might know who to ask."

"Well, we might as well go talk to her," Christine said as she gathered her purse. He thought she was in a rush to get out of here, but he accepted that as he was not happy about being here either, just for a different reason. Dennis opened his car door as Christine opened hers. They walked together up to the door. Dennis rang the doorbell and they waited.

A minute passed before the door opened. A man stood there and looked at them. He was slightly beyond middle age and likely worked a labour job for many years. He looked nothing like Erin Blake.

"I am looking for Erin Blake," Dennis said.

"You must be Dennis Barton," the man said.

"I am," Dennis said.

"I am Erin's uncle," the man said, "And as much as she is supposed to be living here, she isn't."

"Do you know where she is living?" Christine asked.

"I don't ask," the man answered, "She hasn't exactly been in a talking mood for a while now."

"Why?" Dennis asked.

"Her parents were murdered," the man answered, "And she withdrew into herself. I accept her mail and another thing else, but I don't ask her too many questions."

"What about money?" Christine asked.

"I doubt she is worried about that," the man said.

"Thank you for the information," Dennis said.

"Why are you looking for Erin?" the man asked.

"Madison has gone missing," Christine answered.

"Who?" the man asked.

"Thank you for your time," Dennis said before Christine could say anything else, "We are sorry for disturbing you for nothing." Dennis nudged Christine toward the path before following her. The man waited until they were to the car before closing the door.

"Why didn't you explain?" Christine asked, "The more people who know Madison is missing, the more people who will be looking out for her."

"Erin chose not to tell her uncle about Madison," Dennis said, "So, it is not my business to tell him, nor is it yours."

They got into the car.

Dennis climbed up the fire escape, jimmied the lock on the window and climbed into the apartment. The apartment hadn't changed much. It was still a two room apartment, if you counted the bathroom. A counter, a table and a bed filled the main room. The only difference from when Dennis had been here before was the lack of baby furniture. Dennis could hear the shower so he sat down at the table to wait.

It was half an hour wait before the bathroom door opened. The lady who walked out looked exactly like Erin in physical appearance, but the amber eyes looked at him were different. Dennis remembered the blue jeans and black long-sleeved shirt, both being tight enough to show off the body under them but loose enough she could move. The dirty-blonde hair with a slight curl through it and her eye that used to smile all the time were now dead.

"What the hell do you want?" Erin demanded.

"Madison is missing," Dennis said.

"And how exactly is that my problem? You were the one who was supposed to be looking after her," Erin said.

"Madison has been staying with my parents. She disappeared after school yesterday. I was wondering if you knew anything," Dennis said.

"I haven't seen or heard anything of Madison since you took her away. I wouldn't recognize her from any other six-year-old," Erin said, "Why don't you go to the police if she is gone?"

"My mother did as soon as she realized Madison was gone," Dennis said.

"Well, she is obviously not here and I don't know where she is," Erin said, "Why are you still here?"

"Even if you don't know where she is you have the resources to find out," Dennis said. Erin's eyes grew colder.

"And why should I call on my resources? So that you can take her and I never see her again," Erin said, "So, she can be taken in by your parents and raised as if her parents are too busy for her?"

Dennis just about knocked over the chair when he stood up.

"I make time for her; I just don't have the time to watch her all the time," Dennis said.

"Get the hell out of my apartment," Erin said. Dennis went back out the window.

Erin stood there with her arms crossed until she heard Dennis jump from the bottom of the fire escape. She walked over and slumped into the chair he had just occupied.

"And leave me the hell alone," Erin told the now gone Dennis, "You did once, you can do it again and this time, you can't take everything with you."

Erin got up and made herself a sandwich. Once she finished, sighing she stuck it in the fridge. Grabbing her jacket, she climbed out the window and down the fire escape. At the bottom, Erin checked around but Dennis was long gone.

She headed around to the street and headed deeper into the downtown. In the middle of the afternoon, there were plenty of businesses open and people around. Erin ignored most of them as she wandered further. Finally in the middle of the downtown business district, Erin stopped at the steel door of a building lacking in windows. It was hard to tell if the place was open or closed. There was a sign farther along the wall that announced it as Club Weird, but no other explanation. She knocked.

A moment later the door opened and a large man looked her over.

"Hello, Garth," Erin said.

"Long time, Miss. Blake," Garth said with a nod.

"Not interested in the work usually offered," Erin replied, "But I need to talk to a few people about a situation."

"Not everyone is around," Garth said, "But you can talk to who you can find." Garth stepped back and let Erin inside. He closed the door before taking his position in front of it. Erin headed down the dark hallway to the neon lit room at the end. It was dim and smoky as well as full of tables. There was a bar along one side and a jukebox in the corner opposite from the door. The neon lights were spread out along the walls in various shapes and words.

The twenty or so people were scattered around the tables with no more than two at one table. There were bikers, there were those who looked like they had questionable morals, there were those who wore less than was appropriate for this time of day, and then there were those in full business suits. Erin skipped the bartender, who was keeping an eye on her while chatting with a female sitting at the bar, and went straight for the table closest to the jukebox.

The man seated at the table had blond hair hanging in his blue eyes and a few scars on his left cheek. He was wearing dirty jeans and a button-up shirt in need of ironing. There were two empty beer glasses in front of him and one half-full. Erin sat down in the chair across from him.

"What do you need?" the man asked.

"A six-year-old girl named Madison," Erin answered, "She went missing yesterday afternoon school."

"You shouldn't have let her go," the man said.

"Blair," Erin said, "We discussed this before."

"And I still say that you let him walk all over you," Blair said, "Madison is your daughter and he shouldn't have been able to take her away. He doesn't take care of her, he leaves all of her care to his parents."

"You have been watching them," Erin said, "What happened to Madison?"

"She was picked up by a silver SUV," Blair answered, "It belongs to Mr. Robert Barton's former partner, who believes that the Barton family business should be sharing a few million with him rather than Dennis working for his father."

"And that has to do with Madison how?" Erin asked.

"That is your problem," Blair said, "You never bothered with the politics or the relationships. This man is going to find Madison and be the hero, which will mean Robert Barton will be so grateful to have his grandchild back that he will pay the man a large reward for the service."

"But there will be some questions about how he found the child," Erin said.

"Not really," Blair said, "His plan is pretty good that way."

"How do I get Madison and how much is this going to cost me?" Erin asked.

"Why are you worried about it all?" Blair asked, "Madison is in no danger, Dennis will get his daughter back, and Robert can afford the reward."

"I don't know," Erin said.

"He showed up and asked you for help, didn't he?" Blair asked, "You need to learn that those pretty eyes have betrayal on the other end of them whether he means to do it or not. You don't get to be her mother and he gets what he wants without any complications."

"Where is Madison?" Erin asked, "Without any complications."

"I can't get at her until late this evening," Blair answered, "And you can't be there if I am to keep everything I have worked for."

"Fine," Erin said, "Give me a place and time."

"The fast food place on central," Blair said, "About eleven."

"Done," Erin said.

"Take some time with a girl," Blair said, "Because once you give her back, you are never going to see her again."

"See you later," Erin said standing up.

Erin checked her watch as she sat on the cement median in the parking lot of the fast food place. Her coat barely kept her from freezing as the cold kept coming up through her seat. It was twenty after eleven, but Erin was not quite ready to give up on Blair just yet. He rarely let her down. She breathed warm air into her hands in hopes they wouldn't be so cold.

A vehicle turned into the parking lot, but Erin didn't pay it much attention until it parked close to her. Most of the vehicles were interested in the food place and this one didn't seem to have the same objective. It was a red four door sedan. The car was not turned off, but the back door opened. Blair stepped out.

"Good evening," Blair said with a nod as Erin got to her feet.

"You're behind schedule," Erin said.

"I won't charge you," Blair said. He waved someone out

of the car. Out came a small for her age, six-year-old girl with Dennis's facial features and Erin's eyes and hair. She was bundled up in a winter jacket with hat, mittens, and scarf. Her backpack was with her. She looked scared as she looked at Erin, who crouched down to be eye level.

"Hello," Erin said with a smile.

"Hello," Madison said, but she didn't smile back.

"Are you hungry?" Erin asked.

Madison nodded.

"How about we go in and get you something to eat?" Erin asked.

"Okay," Madison answered. Erin held out her hand and Madison took it. Blair got into the car and closed the door. Erin and Madison headed toward the restaurant.

Erin bought Madison's choice for meal before they sat down at one of the tables. Madison ate half her meal before looking up at Erin.

"Am I going to get to go home soon?" Madison asked, "The man said I was going to get to go home soon, but then he didn't come back."

"You will get to go home tomorrow," Erin answered, "It is a little late tonight."

"Grandma never stays up this late," Madison said.

"Exactly," Erin said, "We should wait until she is up in the morning."

"My Dad will be awake though," Madison said.

"Probably best if we wait until your grandma is awake," Erin said.

"You are probably right." Madison sighed before going back to her food.

Erin carried the sleeping girl from the taxi and up the side walk to the house. She dug out her key with her free hand and then unlocked the door. It opened without a noise and Erin stepped inside. She closed it and locked it before headed down the hallway to the guest room. The light from the living room was plenty to see by.

Erin placed Madison down on the bed. She removed the girl's outer wear before putting the blanket over her. Erin closed the door all but a crack after leaving the room. Then Erin went to the living room. Her uncle was sitting on the couch with the television on a low volume.

"What kind of trouble have you brought with you this time?" he asked as Erin sat down in the chair.

"Madison," Erin answered.

"That idiot you used to date came by here the other day looking for a Madison," her uncle said.

"Same Madison," Erin said.

"He have you searching out his missing daughter or something?" her uncle asked.

"Or something," Erin answered.

"Why don't you tell me, girl?" her uncle asked, "You act like there is something to be ashamed of going on."

"That year I disappeared," Erin said, "While I was dating the idiot, as you called him, I ended up pregnant. I told my parents, but they told me not to bother coming back until he had given me a ring. So, I didn't. I had Madison alone instead. Dennis had his own parents suggesting someone of better class, so he had broken it off. About a month after Madison was born, he showed up and took Madison away, According to him, she would be raised better somewhere else. I hadn't seen either of them until today when he showed up looking for her."

"And you're just going to hand her back?" her uncle asked, "You should keep her. After all you are her mother."

"She doesn't know that," Erin said, "It is better she go back to her home."

"You didn't say back to her father," her uncle said.

"She is being raised by her Grandmother," Erin said.

"This was the woman who raised a man to be an idiot and the complete opposite of a gentleman," her uncle said.

"Consider my parents' reaction," Erin said, "They

weren't much better."

"So, who inherits when you get yourself killed?" her uncle asked.

"Whoever is still around at that time," Erin answered.

Erin sat in the dining room and watched as Madison sat at the counter eating a bowl of cereal. Picking up the phone, Erin dialed Dennis' number before putting it to her ear. It rang several times.

"Hello?" Dennis' voice was sleepy.

"I found what you were looking for," Erin said.

"Where?" Dennis was more alert now.

"I'll meet you outside the mall," Erin said, "You can pick her up there. Not your mother, but you. Anyone else there and I'll find someplace else for her."

"That sounds like threat," Dennis said.

"You would know all about those," Erin said.

"And what time am I supposed to be there?" Dennis asked.

"Ten-thirty," Erin answered.

"She is due at school at quarter to nine," Dennis said.

"Then you have to explain to the principal why they need to have better safety for their students," Erin said.

"You don't have to-"

Erin hung up before putting the phone down. Madison had all her attention on her cereal. Erin pushed away any thoughts about keeping the girl.

Erin had them standing in a sunny spot outside the mall entrance, so Madison wouldn't get too cold.

"Are you sure my Dad is coming?" Madison asked as she looked up at Erin.

"Yes," Erin answered giving Madison a reassuring smile, "He said he would be here."

"I know," Madison said, "But sometimes he says he will be somewhere and then doesn't show up. Are you sure you couldn't talk to my grandma?"

"This time he'll be here," Erin said.

Madison turned back to searching the parking lot as she rubbed her mittened hand together. Erin leaned back against the wall and checked her uncle's cellphone. There were no messages.

Erin looked up to scan the parking lot. A silver sports car pulled in and parked near where they were waiting. Dennis stepped out of the vehicle and came over to them.

"Daddy!" Madison held out her arms. Dennis bent down and took Madison into his arms.

"It is good to have you back," Dennis said, "Come on, let's go home."

Madison turned to look at Erin.

"Thank you," Madison said.

"You are welcome," Erin said to Madison. Then Madison took Dennis' hand and let him lead her to the car.

Erin didn't stay to watch them leave. She turned and walked away.

The Best Brownie Recipe

LYRIS

Devon and Luther were dragged across the sand by the pirates. Their wrists and ankles were bound, so there was nothing they could do except try and keep their heads up to avoid getting sand in their faces. They were taken away from the longboats and ocean towards a grove of palm trees. Luther couldn't see anything until they reached the shade of the trees. In the middle of the group of palm trees was a well-built structure. It was made up thick timbers and metal bars. The captain opened the door made up of metal bars so the pirates could throw Devon and Luther inside. Then the door closed with a slight squeak followed by a click of a lock. There was no floor to the building, but just more sand.

"Keep watch on them, Lyris," the captain said.

"Of course, Captain," a female voice responded.

Luther stayed still a moment longer before rolling over on to his front. The building was only one room with nothing inside. There was a window on each side and a door, all made out of metal bars. The rest was timbers, likely from a ship. The sounds and smells were of being close to the water, but the only thing that could been seen out the door were palm trees and a woman sitting at the base of the tree directly opposite from the building. She had her head bent down and was working on something in her lap.

Devon sat up to do the same survey Luther had just done. Luther moved to the back of the building and leaned against it. There was nothing else to do at the moment.

"So, what now?" Devon kept his voice down as he checked to see of anyone was listening.

"I don't know," Luther answered.

"There must be some way out of this," Devon said.

"Likely," Luther said, "But I haven't had enough time to gather any information about this place to know the best way out of here. The best thing to do at the moment is to wait."

"What about the girl?" Devon nodded towards the woman sitting as guard over the little cell.

"If she was that easy to manipulate the captain wouldn't leave her in charge of the prison," Luther said.

"You just don't have the ability with girls that I do," Devon said flashing his best smile. Luther just shook his head. Devon squirmed up to the bars of the door.

Luther closed his eyes and worked to ignore Devon's attempts to flirt with the guard, who seemed to have no trouble ignoring Devon. Devon had yet to learn that not every girl was attracted to him, which was the reason he had to get out of England in a hurry five years ago. A trip they were heading home from when the pirates attacked their ship.

When evening arrived, a pirate arrived with two servings of bread and water. He unlocked the door and left the food before leaving again. He didn't talk to the woman sitting by the tree, nor did he bring her food. She didn't acknowledge his presence but kept working.

Luther moved forward to take his helping of the food and ate before moving back. Devon ate his portion before going back to trying to get the woman to talk to him.

Darkness came without anyone coming back for the dishes. Devon had finally given up for the day and just about asleep. Luther was not letting himself sleep yet as he hoped to learn more about this place.

A light came into view. It got brighter until the lantern and the captain came into view. He set the lantern down beside the woman, who had put aside her work once it was too dark to see. Then he offered her dish of something.

"Any trouble?" the captain asked.

"No more than usual," the woman answered.

"Good," the captain said, "They shouldn't be a problem, but let me know if you have any issues with them."

"Of course," the woman said. The captain left and the woman ate whatever was in the dish. When she was finished, the woman wrapped herself in a blanket from nearby and lay down in the sand to sleep. Luther stayed awake for a little while longer, but there was nothing else happening.

The light coming into the cell was the pink of dawn when Luther opened his eyes. Devon was still sleeping beside the door. Outside the cell, the woman was awake and standing. She was looking out toward the water. Luther wondered what she was looking at, but didn't dare stand up to look out the window in case she noticed him.

As the sun finished rising, the woman went back to her place in the sand and shade. She picked up her project and got back to work. Luther got to his feet slowly. He looked out the window and noted the pirate ship was gone before shuffling over to the corner. When he was done, Luther moved back to his seat and leaned against the wall. He shifted his wrists and tried to find a comfortable position, but it was difficult as the ropes were tight and the knots were well done.

Luther moved over to the door, opposite of where

Devon was lying.

"Can I ask a favour of you?" Luther asked the woman. She looked up at him. She was younger than he had first thought, but her eyes were guarded.

"You can ask," the woman said, "But it is unlikely for you to receive it."

"My wrists are hurting and cramping," Luther said, "Would you please loosen the rope or cut it?"

The woman studied Luther for several minutes as she contemplated his request. He thought for sure she would turn him down as she was the only guard and it would be easier to handle him if he remained tied up.

"I can cut the ropes from your wrists, but you have to keep the ones on your ankles," the woman said, "And you are not to untie your friend."

"I agree to that," Luther said. His ankles were too numb to hurt and he knew untying Devon wouldn't do anyone any good.

The woman took a knife out and moved toward the cell. Luther held his wrists out. She cut the rope off his wrists. Luther shook off the ropes before withdrawing his hands. The woman collected the rope and went back to her spot.

"What is your name?" Luther asked. The woman hesitated a moment as she once again studied him.

"Lyris," she finally answered.

"Thank you, Lyris," Luther said.

"You are welcome," Lyris said. There was a slight smile in her voice, but it never made it her face or eyes. Luther moved back to his spot. Devon was starting to wake up.

Once Devon was fully awake, he started trying to flirt with Lyris. She did not respond at all to him. He might as well be trying to flirt with the palm tree behind her.

"Devon," Luther nudged Devon's foot after an hour of this.

"What?" Devon turned to Luther.

"Give it up," Luther said, "It isn't going to work."

"Have you found another way out of here?" Devon asked.

"No," Luther answered, "But annoying the person guarding our cell isn't going to get us out of here any faster. And if she was going to fall for any of your behaviour, she would have already."

Devon opened his mouth to argue, but something Luther said must have sunk in because he gave up and just leaned back against the wall.

At supper time, several darker skinned individuals arrived with bowls made out of coconut shell. They passed them through the bars to Luther and Devon before leaving one with Lyris. Inside were chunks of coconut in milk, which tasted better than the bread and water from the night before but was not as filling. It was better than going without.

The evening was as uneventful as the day. Luther wasn't as concerned about noticing what was going. The pirates were gone, which meant there were no ships on this island. Everyone else who was here were just as much prisoners as they were. So nothing was going to happen until the pirates got back. Luther drifted off to sleep as he watched the last of the sunlight dance along the sand.

The next week was quiet as the island natives only showed themselves once a day to deliver the evening meal and Lyris working without talking. Devon tried to work out an escape plan, but none of his ideas would have worked. Luther sat quietly and thought about a variety of things.

The pirates arrived late afternoon. It was easy to tell because they made a lot of noise. Half of them must have been drunk from the yelling and singing. But it was all at a distance. After a while two voices came the direction of the cell. They were laughing about something, but Luther couldn't really tell what until they came to the door and within his sight. Between them was a man trussed up. He had definitely more rope around him than either Devon or Luther, but he was also squirming more.

They opened the door and tossed the man inside. When they closed the door, the one pirate noticed Lyris sitting there. He made a step in her direction, but the other pirate pulled him away.

"You bother her and the captain gets upset," the pirate said, "And you don't want that."

The two pirates walked away. The man was trying to talk through the gag. Luther didn't move, but Devon squirmed over and pulled the gaga out.

"Untie me," the man commanded.

"I can't," Devon said holding up his own tied wrists.

"I am Lord Durward," the man yelled, "You can't keep me in here."

"I don't think your shouting is going to change that," Luther said.

"And who are you?" Lord Durward demanded.

"Luther Merrill, Lord of Becin," Luther answered, "And this is Devin, Lord Leland's son."

"Lord Leland would let his son go off where he could be captured by pirates?" Lord Durward asked.

"He said I need to gain experience in the world," Devon said, "Also my older sister is married and likely produce a child who could be his heir."

"Well, what is your plan to get out of here?" Lord Durward asked.

"We don't have one so far," Luther answered.

"You in there," it was a pirate's voice but not one Luther recognized, "Shut up or you will never talk again."

The three men went quiet. The pirate didn't yell at them again. Lord Durward didn't stay quiet for very long. He and Devon started trying to figure out ways to escape. Luther tuned them out. Their plans weren't going to work anyway.

As the evening went on, the pirates got louder as they got more drunk and partied harder. Luther could tell that there were bonfires before he could see the light from the flames after the sun went down. Durward and Devon used the noise to cover the sounds of their plans. Luther tried to sleep, but found there was too much noise. He watched Lyris through the door. She had worked for a long while in the light of the lantern, but was now curling up in her blanket. Luther wasn't sure how she could sleep, however since she lived on the island she was probably used to the noise from the pirates.

Luther must have drifted off to sleep because he blinked and found the sun had come out. And there was a loud boom. Luther stumbled to his feet so he could see out the window. The pirates were either passed out in the sand or still drinking. The noise was coming from a navy ship flying the British flag just off shore. The British ship was blasting their cannons toward the pirate ship. Longboats were headed to the island with uniformed soldiers on them.

Luther looked around the cell. Both Devon and Durward were still sleeping. Outside Lyris sat up briefly. Then she pulled the blanket over herself and moved further back into the shade of the tree. The next blast from the cannons woke Devon and Durward. They sat up.

"What is going on?" Devon asked.

"The British are attacking," Luther answered, "I would advise staying low in case of an errant cannonball." Luther sat down.

"What about the pirates?" Durward asked.

"They are not in good shape due to their partying," Luther answered, "We will likely be free before noon. As long as they don't take out this cell by accident."

There were sounds of metal clashing on metal as the soldiers reached the shore and engaged the pirates. The pirates were aware enough by now to fight back. Aside from the noise, it was impossible for Luther to tell exactly what was happening. He would have gotten to his feet and continued to watch out the window, but he was worried about the cell getting hit and the damage to his person.

Devon and Durward stayed where they were and listened with Luther. Devon occasionally looked like he wanted to say something, but noises from the fighting stopped him. Durward sat at ready as if when the opportunity presented itself he would join the fight, even though he was still tied up. Luther looked over to where Lyris was, but she had not moved.

The cannons stopped, but there were still sword and pistols; also shouting from the combatants. Some people were getting closer to the cell. It didn't sound like the pirates were the ones coming.

Luther reached down and worked at untying his ankles. He knew enough about sailing knots that it didn't take long. Once he was free, Luther kept low as he moved over to where Devon was sitting. The knots were the same making it easy for Luther to undo them and get Devon free. Both moved to where Durward was and started working on the ropes wrapped around him. These knots were slightly different from the ones holding Luther and Devon. Along with Durward squirming, it made it hard to untie him.

There was a knock on the bars of the door. Luther looked up and saw a British soldier working on the lock. He seemed to be having trouble.

"The pirates have the key," Luther said, "Do you have a knife we can use?"

"Here," the soldier said as he pulled out a knife and tossed it through the bars. Luther picked it up and used it to cut through the ropes, while the soldier went off out of sight.

By the time Luther and Devon had Durward free the soldier was back with a key. This time it was easy for the soldier to unlock and open the door. Luther and Devon helped Durward to his feet before they all followed the soldier, who led them through what remained of the battle field. The soldiers were gathering up the pirates who were still alive of which there were few.

Luther saw the captain's body near the water's edge. There was no question that he was dead. Luther wondered who was going to protect Lyris now. He got into a longboat with Devon, Durward, and the soldier. Durward had been talking to soldier and identified Luther and Devon so they weren't going to be taken prisoner or treated poorly.

When they reached the ship, the soldier showed they each to a cabin. Luther didn't stay below and instead he went on deck to watch the cleanup. The soldiers were efficient in their jobs. The pirates were all gathered in one place and tied together. All the loot was collected and placed in a long boat. The natives of the island stayed back and the British soldiers left them alone.

Luther thought Lyris would be safe with the natives, but then he saw her being dragged away from where she had been hiding by one of the soldiers. He had bound her hands behind her back. She was taken to where the pirates were, but she was set apart from them. The pirates paid no attention to her as they were either focused on their own situation or wounds. Luther thought she appeared to have given up, though it was really hard to tell for certain from the distance.

Devon leaned against the railing next to Luther.

"They found her," Devon said, "I thought she had run off."

"She was hiding," Luther said.

"I hope they don't end up sentencing her to death or anything like that," Devon said, "She didn't do anything against us, or likely anyone else who ended up in that prison."

"We should testify at her trial then," Luther said.

"My father would not agree to let me know such a thing," Devon said, "He believes anyone associating with pirates is a pirate and should be treated as such. He would demand she be hung and I shouldn't be anywhere near that trial."

"Then it will just be me at her defence," Luther said.

"Talk to Lord Durward," Devon said, "He may be helpful."

"Or he may hold your father's opinion," Luther said, "I'll talk to him anyway, just in case."

"Well, we are headed home soon," Devon said.

"Your father will be proud that you survived and gained life experience," Luther said.

"It also helps that the fool who wanted to duel with me has been shipped off to Australia for offering to fight the wrong man," Devon said.

"I wouldn't advise you to bring it up," Luther said, "To your father or anyone else. The sooner people forget about the duel the sooner you can go on with life."

"Of course," Devon said.

The men left their conversation there and just watched the soldiers work.

By nightfall everything was loaded on the ship, but the tide was wrong to set sail so everyone waited. Luther had eaten supper with everyone else before wandering below decks. He found the prison cells without difficulty. There were several along one side of the cargo hold. Most of the pirates shared one cell at the end closest to the stairs while Lyris was alone in the furthest cell. Luther wandered down to the cell without appearing to be going anywhere in particular.

Lyris watched him from where she sat on the deck. He could now see her amber eyes, which went well with her dirty-blonde hair and tanned skin. Whatever she had been working had been left on the island and no one was going to go back to get it. Luther looked back at her.

"This will not end well," Lyris said.

"How can going back to England be bad?" Luther asked.

"Why did you leave England?" Lyris asked.

"I was asked to accompany Devon as he escaped from trouble he got into over a girl," Luther answered, "But we were headed back when our ship was attacked. The trouble for him is passed and he can go back to being his father's heir."

"I have no such reason to go back," Lyris said, "In fact, I have all the reasons in the world not to go to England."

"It is unlikely you will be tried as a pirate," Luther said.

"English courts try woman for piracy all the time these days," Lyris said, "They hang them for it too."

"I have not seen you commit any acts of piracy," Luther said.

"What does that matter?" Lyris asked.

"It can be the difference between being charged with piracy and walking free," Luther answered.

"I will never be free while I am on English soil," Lyris said, "That is why I don't want to go back."

Luther waited to see Lyris would say anything else, but she just looked back at him. He wanted to ask while not wanting to pry into her business.

"I am sorry that you have no choice, except to go back," Luther said, "There is no way to leave you behind now."

"If you let me out of here, I can jump off the ship and swim to shore," Lyris said.

"I can't let you out," Luther said.

"I cut the ropes from around your wrists," Lyris said, "You owe me a favour."

"I can't because I don't have a key to get you out," Luther said, "Nor am I good at opening locks without keys. I will have to repay the favour another time."

"Then we have nothing more to discuss at the moment," Lyris said, "You can't help me and I have nothing more to say to you."

"I am sorry," Luther said. He didn't know what else to say and she was firm on her belief that there was nothing more to say. Luther didn't know what else to do. At least she was protected for the moment. Luther wandered back to the stairs as there was nothing more he could do here.

The ship met no others on the journey home, nor did any foul weather make an appearance. So within good time, Luther was standing on deck watching the coast of England get closer. The crew were all busy at their work to bring the ship without problems or delays. Devon and Durward stood with Luther at the railing.

Over the course of the journey Luther had figured out why the pirates had gagged Durward and hogtied him. Also Durward had not seen Lyris or realized she was there. Even now her existence was unknown to him and Luther saw no reason to enlighten him, especially since Devon had not.

Once the ship was docked, Luther watched the soldiers take away the pirates as well as Lyris. Luther had gotten from the captain where they would take Lyris and who to talk to about her situation. Which Luther would do tomorrow, because the rest of today would be taking Devon home before returning to his own house. His house, where the servants were now expecting him because he had sent word ahead to them as well as Lord Leland.

The carriage Luther had sent for arrived. He and Devon left the ship and got inside. Durward had left much earlier as it took much less time for him to gather himself together and be off. The carriage took Luther and Devon directly to the Leland estate as there was nothing for them to gather.

Lady Leland and the butler met them as soon as they stepped out of the carriage. Luther asked the driver to wait as he didn't want to have to call another one when he wanted to leave. Luther was led to the study and given a drink while Devon was whisked away by his mother.

Luther was just about finished his drink when Lord Leland entered the study. He refilled Luther's drink before pouring his own and taking a seat across from Luther.

"I appreciate you keeping Devon safe," Lord Leland

said, "I know you had just come back to England from your property in the colonies. I am sorry that my son's troubles interrupted your return to civilization."

"It is fine," Luther said, "I wasn't exactly relishing my return at the time as there were too many memories of my wife. This time I believe I have come to a place where I can handle them better."

"Your wife died in childbirth, did she not?" Lord Leland asked.

"She fell down the stairs and hit her head," Luther answered, "It caused the death of both her and the child she was carrying. I buried them before I left to develop interests in the colonies. It was too much for me to stay here at the time."

"What are you plans?" Leland asked.

"There was an individual who helped us and may be charged with piracy," Luther said, "And I intend to help that person out. Having Devon testify could help me."

"I thank you for doing the favour of helping my family, but I refuse to have my son associate with anyone charged with piracy," Lord Leland said.

"I figured that would be the case," Luther said, "But I thought I would ask just in case."

Lord Leland launched into his talk about everything that had happened or was happening in England since Luther had left. Luther nodded politely, but really didn't pay much attention to it all. None of the news meant anything to Luther or would affect what he was planning on doing next.

Luther finally managed to leave just before they would have invited him for supper. Had they had a chance he couldn't have refused even though he wanted to get home. The carriage was still waiting for Luther outside. Luther sighed with relief as the Leland estate got smaller and smaller behind him.

Luther sat in his own study with a glass of his own

bourbon and looking at the view from his own window. He might have enjoyed it more, but he had spent much of his morning talking to various officials about Lyris. Despite the fact that no one knew anything about Lyris's role among the pirates, she was found with the pirates so she must have something to do with them. Fortunately he was going to be allowed to testify as was the soldier who had found her. Luther had found the man and the soldier was willing to say how he found Lyris hidden under a blanket instead of fighting with the pirates. There was no point in trying to get any of the pirates to testify because no one would believe a pirate, which also excluded Lyris taking the stand in her own defence.

There was a knock on his study door. Luther thought about sending whoever it was away. He really didn't want to talk to anyone, but it could also be a message from someone he needed to hear from.

"Come in," Luther called. He heard the door open and the butler step into the study.

"A Mr. Vance is here to see you," the butler said, "He claims it is important."

Herbert Vance had been one of the officials from the court who Luther had talked with multiple times over the last several days. Luther turned around and set his drink on the desk.

"Send him in," Luther said.

"Of course," the butler said before leaving. Luther sat up straighter and adjusted his clothing so as to not look like he was slouching.

The door opened and the butler led Mr. Vance in.

"Welcome," Luther said, "Have a seat."

"Thank you," Mr. Vance said. The butler left the room and closed the door behind him.

"What is so important?" Luther asked.

"The girl you wanted to know so much about," Mr. Vance answered, "The trial had been cancelled because the charges have been dropped."

"Why?" Luther asked.

"It happened immediately after Lord Warden visited the judge," Mr. Vance said, "The girl has been placed under Lord Warden's guardianship."

"Why would the judge do that?" Luther asked.

"According to what I have heard the girl is Lord Warden's illegimate daughter," Mr. Vance answered, "And he claimed she had been sent away to protect his family from his affair. Apparently he feels she is his responsibility and he needs to take care of her. So, she'll go to wherever he thinks he can take care of her."

"Then she is gone?" Luther asked.

"She is to go tomorrow," Mr. Vance answered, "It was too late in the day when Lord Warden and the judge finished their discussion. He will send someone tomorrow morning. I thought you should know about all this since you wanted so much information about her situation."

"I do appreciate you coming to tell me all of this," Luther said, "Would it be possible to talk to her before she is taken away?"

"You would have to do it tonight," Mr. Vance said, "And you would likely have to offer the jailer something for his eye sight."

"That can be arranged," Luther said, "What do I owe you for your services?"

"I am paid well for my job," Mr. Vance said, "And so far I have merely done my job."

"Well, if you are ever in need I will try to be available to do what I can," Luther said.

"Thank you for the offer," Mr. Vance said, "I hope to never need it. Would you like me to introduce you to the jailer?"

"Certainly," Luther said, "If you give me one moment, I will be ready to go."

"Take the time you need," Mr. Vance said.

Luther rang for the butler.

Once the butler had escorted Mr. Vance off to the entry way, Luther went and collected his outerwear. Then he went to the entry way. Mr. Vance was surprised at Luther's speed, but didn't say anything. They left Luther's house and headed for the prison.

It didn't take much for the jailer to let Luther in to see Lyris, after Mr. Vance provided the introduction and Luther slipped him some money. Lyris was sitting on the bunk in the empty cell. The cells on either side were empty. Despite it being late, Lyris was still awake.

"What do you want?" Lyris asked.

"I was informed you were placed under the guardianship of your father," Luther said.

"And you want to do that favour you owe me?" Lyris asked.

"What type of favour are you looking for?" Luther answered.

"If not to do me the favour, why are you here?" Lyris asked.

"I am not sure exactly," Luther answered, "But it seems to be that I need to help protect you since the pirate captain died. What favour are you looking for?"

"A knife," Lyris answered.

"I can't get you that," Luther said, "Unfortunately, I have turn down this request as well."

"I guess I should expect as much," Lyris said.

"What would you use the knife for?" Luther asked.

"I would kill myself," Lyris answered, "Because it is better than what I am headed for."

Luther wasn't sure what to say. There had been thoughts in his head about her being protected now and he could move on with his life. But those words suggested otherwise.

"I'm sorry," Luther said.

Lyris didn't give him a verbal response, she just pulled

her knees to her chest and rested her head on them. Luther felt like he a weight had dropped into his stomach, but he didn't know what to do about it. So, Luther walked away from the cell.

Luther sat across for Lord Whitnell as they waited for the Whitnell's housekeeper to finish pouring them tea. Finally each of them had a cup of tea and she left.

"I would offer something stronger," Lord Whitnell said, "But I find myself in trouble after consuming it."

"This early in the day, I am fine with tea," Luther answered.

"Good," Lord Whitnell was relieved, "What can I do for you, Lord Becin?"

"I am looking for information on Lord Warden," Luther answered, "And I was directed to you."

"Lord Warden is my cousin," Lord Whitnell said, "Though I wish it was a much further relationship or not one at all."

"Why?" Luther asked.

"I am ashamed of his behaviours," Lord Whitnell answered, "He is the owner of three brothels and he regularly recruits men to frequent them. He and his wife have three children, who are safe only because he needs them to appear to be respectable. I doubt he and his wife have shared a room, let alone a bed, since their youngest was conceived. He spends most of his nights with the ladies who have nowhere else to go but work for him."

"A girl has turned up, who has been claimed as his illegitmate daughter," Luther said.

"I heard about that," Lord Whitnell said, "And I pity her. She is likely working the same as any other girl he comes across."

"How likely is it that she is his daughter?" Luther asked.

"Very," Lord Whitnell answered, "He has plenty of children outside his marriage, most he doesn't claim."

"Why claim her then?" Luther asked.

"She is the result of a favourite lady of the night," Lord Whitnell answered, "But last anyone heard from the girl was that Lord Warden sold her for a good chunk of money to a man making his fortune in America. Something about the man looking for a mistress to take back with him and the man deciding that only the girl would do."

"And she went back with him," Luther said.

"That is correct," Lord Whitnell said, "There was never any word from him, but there really wasn't one expected. With the story of her being brought up on charges of piracy, I think the man's fate is obvious. And now that she is back in England, her fate is also obvious."

"So, she is back working?" Luther asked.

"Not yet," Lord Whitnell answered, "From what I heard she is not behaving for him and he is working on teaching her the lessons he believes all women need to know. Instead of working she is being kept in a shed at the edge of the property."

"How do you know all this?" Luther asked.

"I pay a couple of his servants to give me information on his activities," Lord Whitnell answered, "Sometimes I think that I can use the information to stop his activities, but so far no opportunity has presented itself. You were trying to help the girl get out of the piracy charge before Lord Warden stepped in to get her back. That is the only reason I am giving you any of this information."

"I don't think I can help with your quest to stop him," Luther said.

"You don't have to," Lord Whitnell said, "But maybe you can help save one person from him. I am willing to start with one and work from there."

"I will need information about the layout of the property, especially the shed," Luther said, "As well as the movement of his men and anyone else who might be an issue."

"What about when you get out?" Lord Whitnell asked, "Lord Warden isn't going to let her go as easily as that when you have made yourself a possible target."

"I will worry about that," Luther answered.

"Probably best," Lord Whitnell said, "The less I know about any sort of rescue or escape plan the less I can tell anyone else. I can get the information to you before the evening is out. I don't know how long he'll keep her there. Probably not long if he finds out people are looking for information about her."

"I thank you for all your help," Luther said.

"As I have said, I am glad to help," Lord Whitnell said, "My cousin's behaviour disgusts me and I feel it is my job to do what I can against him."

Luther had the driver stop the carriage close to the wharf, where he made an inquires with the officials about which ships were leaving in the next twenty-four hours. He visited each captain and spoke to them for a few moments. Finally he found one leaving within his time frame and heading toward America, who accepted a handshake and a verbal agreement to take Luther and Lyris on. Then Luther headed home to wait for the information Lord Whitnell agreed to send him.

There was a knock at the door. Luther looked up at the interruption of his thoughts. He glanced around. It was late afternoon.

"Come in," Luther called. The door opened and the butler stepped inside.

"What is it?" Luther asked.

"There is a gentleman asking to see you," the butler said, "He is a notary."

"Send him in," Luther said.

"Are you leaving again, Lord Becin?" the butler asked.

"I am," Luther answered, "And I am not likely to come

back this time."

"Who will you leave in charge of the estate?" the butler asked.

"My uncle has several children," Luther answered, "One of them will likely be given that charge."

"That part of the family was castout for very good reasons," the butler said.

"That is why I need to talk to this notary," Luther said, "He knows enough of the family tree to help find someone who is closer to the immediate family and not a part which has been tossed."

"I will show him in immediately," the butler said.

"Thank you," Luther said.

The moon was a slight sliver in the sky. It didn't provide much light, but there was plenty from other sources enabling Luther to see the outline of the shed. He could not see any people around and Lord Whitnell's information said there wasn't any guards, just a lock.

Luther moved forward. Nothing else moved. He continued toward the shed and reached it without anyone stopping him. Luther took out the key that had come with the information. It slid easily into the lock and turned. There was a slight creak as the door opened, but not loud enough to attract attention.

Luther looked inside the shed. Lyris was lying against the back wall of the small space. Even in the dark, Luther could see the new tears in her clothing from where she had been beaten and whipped. He moved closer and she didn't move. Her eyes were closed, but he found she was breathing.

As gently as he could, Luther lifted her up. She moaned softly and her eyelids fluttered briefly, however she didn't open them. Luther maneuvered to avoid bumping Lyris against the sides of the doorway. He closed the door with his feet before moving away from the shed.

Luther hadn't gotten far when he heard several people coming towards the shed. While being careful of Lyris and her pain, Luther ducked behind a clump of bushes and kneeled down. He hoped he could not be seen despite the thinness of the cover. The people came toward the shed.

"Are you sure you heard something?" the first voice demanded.

"I am sure," a meeker second voice replied.

"Everything looks fine," the first voice said. The men wandered around and checked for whatever made the noise. They passed the bushes where Luther was hiding, but they didn't see him. After not finding anything, the men headed back toward the house.

They had barely gone more than a few steps when Lyris moaned from the pain. Luther shifted Lyris to try and make her more comfortable. The men stopped and one turned back toward the shed.

"Should be check that out?" the second voice asked.

"No," the first one replied, "She isn't going anywhere."

They turned back around and headed for the house. Luther stayed still until they were inside. Then he carefully got to his feet, while trying not to jostle Lyris. He checked the street before crossing it.

A few streets over, a carriage waited for him. The driver looked questioningly at him, but opened the door for him. Luther placed Lyris on the bench before sitting on the one across from her.

"The wharf," Luther instructed the driver.

"Right away, Governor," the driver said before getting up into his seat. There was a lurch as the carriage started moving forward. Luther checked to make sure it didn't bother Lyris much. Her eyes were half-hooded by her lids, but she didn't say anything. Luther took a blanket he had left on the seat beside him and draped it over her.

"I thought about how I would get a knife to you, but there didn't seem to be any way," Luther said, "So, I thought I would get you out of there instead."

"You think that will stop him?" Lyris's voice was very rough.

"I think it will slow him down," Luther said, "Because I doubt the alarm will sound before we leave the city."

"Where?" Lyris asked.

"Wherever the ship is going," Luther answered, "From there we'll figure it out."

"Why?" Lyris asked opened her eyes and looked at him.

"Because I feel I need to help you," Luther answered, "I never wanted you to be found on the island by the soldiers. I was ready to defend you against the charges of piracy. I thought you were safe until you asked for the knife. Then I couldn't stop until I helped out of that situation as well. It seems to be my doom to help people I should leave to their own fate"

"What about your children?" Lyris asked as she sat up. She was moving tenderly.

"I have no children," Luther answered, "My wife died before we could have any children and I have no interest in getting married again."

"How long to the ship?" Lyris asked as she leaned against the side of the carriage.

"Soon, I hope," Luther answered.

They were quiet as the carriage rolled through streets of Brighten. The smell of the sea got closer as they went. Finally the smell and sounds of the wharf were right outside the windows. The carriage stopped and the driver opened the door. Luther got out first and offered Lyris his hand. She accepted the help as she carefully stepped down.

Luther paid the driver before escorting Lyris to the ship. The captain was waiting at the top of the gangplank.

"You are close to being late," the captain said.

"I am sorry," Luther said, "When are we leaving?"

"As soon as you are on board," the captain said.

"Good," Luther said. Luther and Lyris moved passed the

captain. They went to the railing at the front of the ship, while the captain brought up the gangplank. Soon the captain was barking orders to get the ship under way. Luther watched at Lyris faced toward the open ocean and the relief on her face. Luther had only one thought. She was finally safe.

NOTES

Both Stuck in the Elevator and The Professor are both inspired by my viewing of the TV show Doctor Who. The first one comes from the first season which features the ninth doctor. The second story comes from watching the David Tenant seasons of Doctor Who.

STUCK IN THE ELEVATOR

I pressed the button for the sixth floor and watched the elevator doors close. I leaned against the back of the elevator and sighed. One short meeting was all I needed for my boss to be happy enough to give me a raise.

There was a ding and the doors slid open, but it was only the second floor. I looked up to see three people. All of them were obese and they were all laughing like the typical movie villain, but stopped at the sight of me. They shuffled on to the elevator and turned their backs to me. I was okay with that because I needed to keep a lower profile while in the building.

It was loud, it stank, and it came from the one in front of me. I tried not to gag. The fart was not silent, but it was deadly. Though it didn't smell quite like a fart, more like bad breath. The people in front of me stifled their giggles.

Then all three of them let loose. I fought for air as greyness entered my vision. The three giggled again, but I think it might have been a reaction to a sound I made as I tried not to faint. Though the air down there might have been safer.

Finally the elevator went ding and the doors slid open.

The three people stepped out and headed down the hallway. I swear they were still giggling. The doors closed. I struggled a moment longer, but the greyness took over and I passed out.

The Best Brownie Recipe

THE PROFESSOR

Doctor Smith looked up from his paperwork when the room shook. There was nothing to suggest the problem as he put down his pen. As he was getting to his feet, Nurse Jones came to the doorway.

"What is it?" Doctor Smith asked.

"We are being attacked," Nurse Jones answered.

"By what?" Doctor Smith asked, "We are a hospital and no danger to anyone."

"Come see," Nurse Jones answered. She headed down the hallway. Doctor Smith followed her. His office was at the end of a hallway with patient rooms on either side all the way down. At the end was another hallway. This hallway had windows along one side and more patient rooms on the other side. Doctor Smith was not worried about the shaking of the building disturbing the patients, since most of them were kept under heavy sedation due to acting out as a result of their mental issues.

They stopped at the large window at the end of the hallway. Doctor Smith looked out. At first, the sun set made it difficult to see anything beyond large, dark shapes surrounding the building. Then Doctor Smith's eyes adjusted to the lighting and he could see what was attacking them.

They were six feet tall, four feet across hand to hand, and deep brown. Their eyes and mouths were white. The three 'buttons' down their fronts were a random selection of five colour choices. They were giant gingerbread man and there were dozens and dozens of them.

The cookies were banging on the doors and windows. As it was after hours, all the doors had been locked and the bars on the windows were put in when the hospital switched the types of patients it housed. It was hard to tell, but Doctor Smith thought the cookies might be crumbing as they pushed.

"Will they be able to get in?" Nurse Jones asked. The fear in her voice made it close to breaking.

"I do not know," Doctor Smith answered. He was worried, but relied on his training to keep himself calm.

The shaking stopped as the vehicle stopped. Alice let go of the armrest. The Professor waited until the vehicle had definitely come to a stop before moving.

"Where are we?" Alice asked.

"A hospital," the Professor answered after consulting the vehicle's instruments.

"Let's go see why," Alice said opening the door.

"That would be why we're here," the Professor replied before following her.

They were in the custodian supplies closet. Alice was already pulling on the door. It opened easily. The Professor barely managed to catch up with her before the door closed.

They were now in a long hallway with a double-door in the middle to their left and what appeared to be a staircase at the far end. The Professor stopped at the doors and pushed one open to peek inside. He withdrew his head and they continued down the hallway.

"Well?" Alice asked.

"Morgue," the Professor answered, "Nothing alive in there and no signs of trouble."

"Good," Alice said.

They reached the stairs and started up. They had reached a landing when the building shook, but not for very long.

"I wonder what that could be," Alice said.

"Let's keep going and find out," the Professor said.

They hurried up the next sets of stairs. This brought them into the main reception area with the front doors on one side and a large staircase leading to the second floor. There were chairs against the walls as if waiting for people to fill them. Between the chairs and the staircase, there was a desk with an empty receptionist's chair.

"Strange," the Professor said, "I thought someone would be here to greet us."

There was banging on the front door. The Professor and Alice looked towards the windows. Enough sunlight was left for them to see the shapes were pounding on the bars. The Professor stepped closer while Alice stepped back.

"And who are these?" the Professor asked as he peered out the window.

"Get back," a female voice called. There was the sound of two people's footsteps hurrying down the staircase. The Professor turned to see a doctor and nurse coming down the stairs.

"Back away from the windows, sir," the doctor said. The Professor backed away from the window.

"Who are they?" the Professor asked.

"The Gingermen," the doctor answered.

"And who or what is the Gingermen?" the Professor asked.

"I don't know," the doctor said, "I have heard of them from colleges, we have never seen them before today. They are said to kill anyone they touch."

"Well, it can't be good," the Professor said.

"Who are you?" the doctor said, "How did you get in

here with them all out there?"

"I am sorry," the Professor said, "I'm the Professor and this is Alice. We are travellers and were called here because someone needed help."

"We certainly seem to need it," the nurse said, "I am Nurse Jones and this is Doctor Smith. We are the night shift here at the hospital. Us and the night guard."

"Where is the night guard?" Alice asked looking around.

"He was supposed to be at the desk," Doctor Smith said looking towards the desk.

The Professor went to the desk and looked around it. There was a hat and a pile of brown chunks. The Professor picked up a piece the size of his index finger. He smelled it and then licked it.

"What is it?" Doctor Smith asked.

"Gingerbread," the Professor answered as he put the piece back in the pile before dusting off his hands.

"One of those things must have gotten in," Nurse Jones said.

The Professor picked up the hat.

"That is the night guard's hat," Doctor Smith said, "He must have left it behind when he went to do his rounds."

"I've never seen him without it," Nurse Jones said, "But I suppose he may have left it."

"Interesting," the Professor said as he placed the hat on the desk.

The glass shattered in the window closest to the door. Everyone backed away quickly, but the Gingermen had not figured out how to get themselves through the bars despite being thin enough.

"I think we best retreat to a more secure locations," Doctor Smith said, "Before they figure out how to get through the bars."

"I think so," the Professor said.

The four headed up the staircase at a suitable speed for getting away from Gingermen trying to get in the window.

They reached the top of the stairs before turning around to look. The Gingermen were starting to figure out how to get through the window whole. There were a few already through, but they were missing arms, or legs, or even heads.

The group went through the door at the top of the staircase. Doctor Smith and Nurse Jones closed the door with Doctor Smith locking it. They all stood there and caught their breath.

"Anyone have any ideas how to get rid of giant gingerbread cookies?" Doctor Smith asked.

"Tea," Alice answered, "Tea would soften them."

"Genius," the Professor said, "Where is the kitchen?"

"Down there," Nurse Jones said as she pointed down one hallway

"Go," the Professor said, "Make as much tea as you can and I will defend this position."

Alice and Nurse Jones started towards the kitchen. Doctor Smith, however, remained where he was.

"You aren't likely to survive alone," Doctor Smith said, "I will help."

Once inside the kitchen, Alice and Nurse Jones started going through the cupboards. They got out the largest pots they could find for the burners they had available. Alice filled them at the sink. Nurse Jones put them on the burners. When that was done, all they could do was wait. Alice stayed near the door where she would watch the Professor and Doctor Smith through the small window.

As soon as the pots can to the boil, Nurse Jones put the tea bags in. She made sure there were two tea bags for every three cups of water. Then she put the lids back on the pots without the heat being on.

Alice watched the door at the top of the stair burst open and Gingermen start toward the Professor and Doctor Smith. Each man had armed himself with what could be found in such a short time and easy accessibility. The Professor was swinging a mop and Doctor Smith a hammer.

"The Gingermen are getting through," Alice said, "How much longer on the tea?"

"Four minutes," Nurse Jones answered.

The Gingermen were coming through the door as if there was an unlimited supply of them. Doctor Smith was knocking hands of the cookies along with making cracks when he could. The Professor was doing similar, but he had a much longer reach with his weapon and was able to keep the cookies farther away. There were several times Doctor Smith came close to being touched by a cookie. A few of those times, it was the Professor who hit the Gingermen and stopped anything from happening to Doctor Smith.

"They may not last that long," Alice said.

"It is hardly proper tea if you don't let it steep," Nurse Jones said.

Alice watched the fight while Nurse Jones watched the time. The Professor and Doctor Smith fought with whatever weapons they could find. The problem with gingerbread is the hardness of the cookie, making it difficult to break them. Or pieces would break off, but the body kept coming.

"It is ready now," Nurse Jones said finally, "How do we get it out there?"

"You take one side and I'll take the other," Alice said, "We toss at the largest groups we can and then come back for the next pot."

"All right," Nurse Jones said.

They each took an oven mitt. They picked up the first pot by the handles. They ran down the hallway. The Professor and Doctor Smith were pushed in the direction of the kitchen by the Gingermen.

"Duck," Alice shouted. The Professor pulled Doctor Smith with him as he went down. The women tossed the tea over the men's head and into the onrush of cookies. The tea hit the Gingermen and caused them to stagger a bit. After a second several started forward again, but they had absorbed too much tea and started to crumb. The ones behind tried to avoid the puddle of tea on the floor and keep attacking.

"Another one," Alice shouted at Nurse Jones. Nurse Jones nodded and they hurried back to the kitchen for the next pot.

When they came back out, the Professor and Doctor Smith had pushed the Gingermen back to the staircase. Alice and Nurse Jones tossed the batch of tea down the staircase at the Gingermen. When the tea hit, several Gingermen hissed before folding over with sogginess. They fell back into their comrades and cause the moisture to spread.

The Professor and Doctor Smith followed the destruction down. They beat back the last few who had come through the window. And then there were no more enemies left to fight.

"We did it!" Alice said.

"We did it!" the Professor replied.

Doctor Smith and Nurse Jones smiled at each other. Nurse Jones accepted a hug from Alice.

"Thank you so much for your help," Doctor Smith said shaking the Professor's hand, "We would have been overrun without you."

"Not a problem," the Professor said, "Should be the last of that problem for a while."

The four got started on cleaning up the mess. In doing so, they boiled all the crumbs in water before getting rid of them just to be safe. Finally the Professor and Alice said their good-byes and headed back down to where they had parked their vehicle.

They had reached the custodian's closet when the Professor's watch peeped.

"What is it?" Alice asked.

"How do you feel about shrubberies?" the Professor asked as they got into the vehicle. A slight breeze and the vehicle was gone.

The Best Brownie Recipe

B. Heather Mantler

WHY MATTHEW DIDN'T STAY OUT

Matthew sipped his beer while watching his friend join the woman who had been making eyes at him further down the bar. Then Matthew turned back to the bar. Doug nudged Matthew's elbow. Matthew turned to him.

"What?" Matthew asked.

"Her," Doug nodded toward someone on the dance floor. Matthew turned around and looked. The woman was easy to spot since she was looking right at him and smiling. She was wearing painted on jeans and a red halter top. Her brown hair hung down to her elbows and she wore a gold chain with some kind pendent.

Matthew turned back to his drink and took another sip.

"What is wrong with her?" Doug asked.

"Not interested tonight," Matthew answered.

"How can you not be interested in that?" Doug asked, "Especially since you haven't taken anyone home in weeks. Why could you not be interested?"

"I'm just here because I agreed to come for a couple drinks," Matthew answered, "That is all I am here for."

"You have gone weird," Doug said before patting Matthew on the back before moving on. Matthew shook his head before taking another sip of his drink.

He was in the last half of the beer when he felt a hand on his shoulder as the woman sat down on the stool next to his.

"Hello, Handsome," the woman purred.

"Not interested," Matthew replied.

"Sure you are," the woman said moving her hand down his hand.

"No, I'm really not interested," Matthew said. He tossed back the rest of his beer before paying the bartender for his drink. Matthew brushed off the woman's hand and got to his feet. He left the bar, feeling the woman's eyes still on him.

There was a cab out front with a man getting out and on his way inside the bar. Matthew caught the door before it could finish closing and slide in. The driver glanced back.

"Where to, Mister?" the driver asked.

"Bluetown village apartments," Matthew answered.

"Right away, Mister," the driver said. He took his foot off the brake and the taxi pulled away from the curb.

"Early night, Mister?" the driver asked.

"I went to drink with my buddies," Matthew answered, "They got distracted and aren't likely to notice that I left. And I was starting to get attention I wasn't interested in. I figured I might as well head home."

"That is very understandable," the driver said, "Better to leave before any trouble starts."

"Exactly," Matthew said.

"I would do the same, but my motive would be my beautiful wife," the driver said, "I don't like leaving her to stay at home by herself while I have drinks with my buddies."

"She must be a lucky woman," Matthew said.

"No," the driver said, "I am a lucky man for having her in my life and I don't want to do anything that would cause her to leave me."

"She must be okay with you working nights," Matthew said.

"She understands," the driver said, "And she sleeps while I am at work. Occasionally she has her sister come over to keep her company."

"You must really trust her family," Matthew said, "I've known a few relationships where that would be harmful."

"I get along with my in-laws well enough that they have accepted me," the driver said, "And effort on their part would do more harm to their relationship with my wife."

"And relationship to envy," Matthew said. The driver pulled over to the curb in front of the apartment complex.

"I call it love," the driver said with a smile as he glanced back to Matthew. Matthew counted out the money and a little extra.

"One of the best feelings in the world," Matthew smiled back as he offered the driver the money, "Good night."

"Good night," the driver said with a nod. Matthew got out of the taxi and went to the door to the apartment complex. Once he was inside, Matthew saw the taxi pull away and then headed up to his apartment.

Matthew closed the door to his apartment and locked it behind him. Inside he slipped off his jacket and draped it over a kitchen chair before pulling off his boots. He left those next to the chair. Matthew stopped briefly at the sink to have a drink of water. Then Matthew headed down the hallway and went into his bedroom.

The blonde lady was lying across the bed with the sheet slipping down off her naked form. Her eyes were closed, but Matthew felt that he had woken her when he entered. She rolled on to her side and the sheet slipped further down to show her nipple. Matthew sat down on the other side of the bed. She opened her sleepy green eyes.

"Hey," her voice was rough, "I thought you were going to stay out longer."

"I would have," Matthew said, "But the guys decided to

do other things and I didn't feel like joining them in that behavior. I would rather be here instead."

"Their loss," she smiled as she reached up to him.

"If you say so," Matthew smiled back as he leaned down to her.

The Best Brownie Recipe

NOTES

John Doe was originally titled John Smith. It was a story I wrote for an English class I took at the College of New Caledonia. Several of the scenes were inspired by various exercises done in class.

JOHN DOE

One day...

He stopped at the wall and looked at the generic painting. The fields were merely brush strokes of yellow and brown to him. The scene as a whole was foreign to him as a cheap hotel room. He turned and walked back across the room. This side had an electric fireplace, but there was no reason for it to be turned on today. He stopped and glanced at his wristwatch.

She was late, he thought to himself as he turned back around and started across the room again.

Half way across there came a knock at the door. He stopped and headed for the apartment door. Reaching it, he hesitated a moment. He reminded himself that it could not be Melissa at the door, but his gut told him that it was not the woman he was waiting for.

The thought came up that he should ask the manager to put in a peephole. With a few hundreds slipped to him the manager wasn't likely to even ask why.

The man took the chain off the door before turning the knob. He opened the door enough that he could see who was there and still have enough time to slam it shut. There were three men standing outside the door. Two of the men were in suits and one in the navy uniform of a police officer. The man opened the door wider.

"Can I help you?" the man asked.

"Are you John Smith?" the man in the suit on the right asked as he held up a police badge.

"Yes," the man answered.

"You're under arrest for murder," the other detective said bringing out a set of handcuffs.

The man stood there as the detective put the handcuffs on him. Then he was led out by the detectives. They led him around the corner of the hallway. The elevator and the hallway in front of it were blocked off with yellow crime scene tape.

As the police led the man toward the stairs, he glanced at the scene with disinterest before going back to concentrating on where he was being led.

A couple hours later...

The detective stared at the officer and the lab technician.

"You're telling me, the man in there, has no fingerprints, and no face or DNA in any database," the detective asked pointing to the man on the other side of the glass.

"The whole palm of his hand has been burned," the officer said, "We can't get fingerprints or palm prints."

"We checked every database and couldn't find a match to his DNA," the lab technician said, "So, we ran his picture against all the databases and here were no results."

"So, all we know about this guy is that his name is John Smith," the detective said, "And we only know that because it was the name on the apartment lease. He could be anyone."

"We'll see if we can't narrow that down," the lab technician said, "We will check his clothes and the apartment."

"John Smith did ask that his lawyer be called," the

officer said, "He hasn't said anything about not talking."
The officer offered a business card to the detective. The
detective took the card and looked at it. The detective
recognized the lawyer's name. He was a good lawyer and a
good guy. He had worked for the prosecution many times.
He didn't have a list of scumbag clients, nor did he like to
represent people like that.

"Call him," the detective said handing the business card
back. Then the detective headed for the interrogation room.

A minute later...

He tapped his fingers on the table. The clock ticked on
the wall behind him. Somewhere in the distance there were
echoes of men yelling at each other. A large black fly was
repeatedly attacking the bare light bulb that hung over him.

A mirror encompassed the wall in front of him. It
reflected the metal table that was bolted to the floor, the
two chairs built for practicality not comfort, and bare grey
walls.

Tick, buzz, bam, bam, tick, bam, buzz, tick, tap, tap,
tick, bam, tap, tick, buzz, tap, bam, tick.

He stopped tapping the table and smoothed his hair back
with that hand. He watched the mirror to check that every
strand was in place. He dropped his hand back to the table.
He lifted his finger to start tapping again.

The door opened and the detective stepped inside before
closing the door behind him. The detective had a file and an
envelope in his hand. The detective set them on the table
before sitting down in the opposite chair. The detective
straightened the file folder before picking up the envelope
and pouring the contents on the table. The items scattered
themselves across its surface. The detective shook the
envelope again just to make sure that everything was on the
table.

"What happened, John?" the detective asked, "Who was
she? And why did you shove her down the elevator shaft?"

"I didn't shove her down an elevator shaft," he replied. He stopped himself from reaching for the rusted screw that had come to rest near his hand. He looked at the detective rather than the objects.

"So, what happened?" the detective asked.

He glanced at the objects on the table before looking back up at the detective.

"She used to be my mistress," he said, "I opened the apartment door to find her standing there. She was not supposed to be there because I told her that the relationship was over two days ago. I asked her how she got passed the doorman and she said that she had come in through the basement window." He pushed the screws into a pile.

"Why did she show up?" the detective asked.

"She wanted our relationship to continue," he answered, "She said that she would tell my wife about us if I refused. She was going to take the pictures of us to my wife as proof of the relationship." He picked up the slip of paper from the photo store. "She said that the photos were hidden somewhere safe."

"What happened next?" the detective asked.

"I explained again to her that the relationship was over as I escorted her back to the elevator," he answered, "I gave her the keychain and nun figurine as gifts because I knew that she collected religious items. She tried to give me the cologne, but I refused it. It was cologne she enjoyed the smell of and not the kind I usually wear."

"Did you go to a photographer for the photographs?" the detective asked picking up the business card.

"No," he answered, "She was a model. The card was probably from her latest job."

"So, you are standing in front of the elevator doors," the detective said, "What happened?"

"We weren't at the elevator yet," he answered, "the apartment was on the other side of the building from the elevator. We were talking as we walked. When we came into view of the elevator I saw that the doors were open and slowed down. She didn't, she was angry at me and still was threatening me. She said that if I didn't keep seeing her then she was going to tell my wife.

"They must have been doing work on the elevator because there was an extension cord on the floor in front of the elevator. She wasn't looking where she was going and tripped over the cord. She fell into the elevator shaft. The elevator must have been at the basement floor."

"And you just walked away?" the detective asked.

"I figured that the repairman would find her and report it," he answered, "Then she wouldn't be connected back to me."

"Through the doorman we connected her to you," the detective said, "What was her name?"

"Melissa," he answered, "We never told each other our last names and I never tried to figure out what hers was."

"Did she call you John?" the detective asked.

"Yes," he answered.

"Does your wife call you John?" the detective asked.

"You can direct the rest of your questions to my attorney," he answered.

Half an hour later...

The detective was standing beside his desk reading a file when the lawyer entered the police station. The lawyer went over to the detective.

"How are you, Detective?" the lawyer asked offering his right hand.

"Well, how about yourself?" the detective shook hands with the lawyer.

"I just got back from a week off," the lawyer answered.

"Stay at home and relax, or get away for awhile?" the detective asked.

"My in-laws were having a family reunion," the lawyer answered, "The good times last about three days and then the rest of the time is waiting until we can come home."

"At least you get three days," the detective said.

"True," the lawyer said, "How is my client?"

"He gave us his story, but he won't tell us anything about who he is," the detective answered, "What do you know about him?"

"Not much," the lawyer answered, "All his bills are sent to John Smith, all the cheques are signed John Smith, but his name isn't John Smith, I don't know what his name is and he isn't willing to tell me."

"I'm surprised he has a lawyer," the detective said.

"A former mistress was suing him for child support," the lawyer said, "He hired me to prove that the child wasn't his, which only took a DNA test. I think he has had a vasectomy, but he won't admit to anything that might require giving out information about himself."

"Well, we can't find him in any database," the detective said, "Fingerprints, DNA and photo came up with nothing."

"What is he in for?" the lawyer asked, "The officer didn't specify."

"Pushing his latest mistress down an elevator shaft," the detective answered.

"My guess," the lawyer said, "is that he broke up with her and she wasn't interested in letting go. He killed her because she inconvenienced him. Now he is hoping to deal with this and move on with his life."

"The charges aren't going away," the detective said.

"I know," the lawyer said, "He's in the interrogation room?"

"Yes," the detective answered. The lawyer headed into the back.

The next day...

The lab technician came into the police station and went over to the detective's desk. The detective looked up at him.

"What did you find?" the detective asked.

"Nothing as to who he could be," the lab technician answered, "His clothes don't hold any clues and the apartment is for the most part clean."

"For the most part?" the detective asked.

"The bed has plenty of DNA samples on it," the lab technician answered, "It looks like it hasn't been washed for the length of time that John Smith has been renting the apartment. We found his DNA as well as the woman from the elevator. There was newer female DNA sample and several older female DNA samples."

"Well, that answers what he has the apartment for," the detective said, "Anything useful?"

"No," the lab technician answered, "No matches in any databases."

"Anything else?" the detective asked.

"There was a message from another lab," the lab technician answered, "John Smith's DNA is a match to an unsolved case that didn't come up in our search. The lab is going to send over the case file as soon as possible."

"Did they tell you anything about this case?" the detective asked.

"The victim is currently known only as Jane Doe number 1387692," the lab technician answered, "The DNA is never been matched to any missing person. Despite finding the body within twenty four hours of the murder, they can't get fingerprints or use facial reconstruction. The person that called warned me about the case. Something about the fact, that every bone in the woman's body had been broken without her being crushed with something heavy."

"That doesn't sound good," the detective said.

"I'll bring the case file over as soon as I get it," the lab technician said.

"Thank you," the detective said. The lab technician turned and left the police station.

The next morning...

The lab technician entered the police station and took the file over to the detective. The lab technician didn't say anything, he just left the file with the detective. After flipping through the report, the detective reached the pictures. For the first time in his fifteen years as a police officer, he lost his lunch over crime scene photos. According to the report, John Smith's DNA was all over the murder weapon as well as the body.

Two months have passed...

The television screen flickered once before it came up with the bright blue screen. The prosecution put the video tape into the VCR. The screen flickered again before the blue was replaced by a fairly clear picture of an apartment building hallway. It was empty of people, but the elevator door was open and there was a cord stretched out in front of it. A moment of empty hallway went by before John Smith and Melissa Russell came into view. There was no sound coming from the television. John had Melissa's elbow in a tight grip as he led her down the hallway. She didn't look happy and kept trying to twist away, but he wasn't letting go. They looked to be arguing with each other. Melissa didn't notice that they were headed for an open elevator shaft until she was on the edge. John shoved her forward. She could not keep her balance and fell. John stood there and looked over the edge. Then he nodded to himself before turning around and going back down the hallway. He walked out of the frame looking like nothing had happened. The prosecution stopped the tape and ejected it from the VCR before turning off the television.

Three weeks later...

The jury entered the court room in a single file line. They went to their seats and sat down. Finally they had all entered and the guard had closed the door. Everyone else was already settled and waiting. The judge waited until the jury was settled.

John was about the only person in the whole courtroom who was relaxed. His lawyer wanted to snap at him and get him to quit the self-confident attitude. The lawyer knew that John was not going to get out of here scott-free. But he remained silent because that was what was needed at this time.

"Madam Foreman, have you reached a verdict?" the judge asked. The jury foreman stood up.

"Yes, your honour," she answered, "We the jury find the accused guilty of first degree murder in the cases of Melissa Russell and Jane Doe number 1387692."

"Thank you," the judge said, "The sentencing hearing will be tomorrow at ten o'clock." The judge banged the gavel against the base.

"All rise," the court clerk called. Everyone in the court got to their feet. The judge stood up and left the courtroom. The lawyer didn't look at John as he collected all the papers and put them away in his briefcase. The sheriff came over to put the handcuffs back on John. John said nothing and went willingly. The lawyer glanced up at him as he was being led away. John had remained calmed and still had that confident air. The lawyer shook his head as he got ready to leave the court room.

The next morning...

The lawyer sat there at the table as he waited. The sheriff brought John in and they went to the table. The sheriff undid the handcuffs before moving away. John gave off a calm air, but it was not as relaxed today.

"We can appeal," the lawyer told John, "I can have the process started immediately after this hearing is finished."

"Will that change the outcome of this whole process?" John asked.

"With the evidence the prosecution has," the lawyer replied, "not likely."

"Then there is no other point to appealing, aside from wasting everyone's time?" John asked.

"Well, there are small chances that things will change," the lawyer answered, "Most people try."

"I have no interest in wasting time," John said, "Do not bother with appealing."

"Okay," the lawyer said.

"All rise," the court clerk said. Everyone in the court room stood up. The judge came into the courtroom and sat down in his chair. The rest of the people took their seats.

"This is the sentencing hearing of John Smith," the court clerk announced, "Case number 736958." The court clerk sat down.

"John Smith," the judge said.

"Yes, your honour," John stood up.

"A jury of your peers has found you guilty of two counts of first degree murder." the judge said, "Due to the severity of the crimes, I sentence you to death. Do you have a method you prefer?"

"Lethal injection," John answered.

"You are hereby sentenced to death by lethal injection," the judge banged the gavel on the base.

Two years later...

John set the tray down before sitting down in the chair. He inhaled through his nose and sighed in contentment. John picked up his utensil and started to eat.

The poached eggs were cooked to the point where the yolks weren't runny, but still retained their flavour. There was no excess water on them either. The eggs were as perfect as the ones he had been served at the diner he stopped at four years ago. If it hadn't been for his car troubles he would have bypassed the diner completely. But he was starving and his car was going to take an hour or two so he went inside. He had wiped off the seat before he sat down, wiped off the table before the waitress came over with the menu, and wiped off the cutlery before his food arrived. But the poached eggs had turned out to be perfect.

The bacon was crisp without being burnt. The pieces were still dripping with grease. They reminded him of the first night he had spent at his girlfriend's house. She had made him bacon and eggs the next morning. She had over cooked the bacon that morning. She had blamed him for distracting her. That morning he hadn't minded over-cooked bacon

The hash-browns were under salted, but he left the ketchup packets alone that were on the tray. It was better to have under salted hash-browns than desecrate them with ketchup. He had hated ketchup since the incident in high school. The person he had considered his best friend had dumped a container of ketchup over his head right in front of the girl he had a crush on. She declined his invitation to the school dance, even after he had cleaned up, the whole episode was in the yearbook. He wished that there were salt packets provided rather than ketchup packets. That would make more sense to him.

The toast might have been crisp at some point before the butter was slathered on. He put the toast to one side of the tray and focused his attention on the pancakes. The pancakes tasted wonderful. Completely unlike his mother's pancakes used to be. His mother's pancakes always tasted like baking powder despite having blueberries in them. But he never dared to say anything and he always ate them as if he loved them. He didn't have much of choice at that point in his life.

The door opened and the chaplain entered the room before the door closed behind him. The chaplain smiled at John.

"How is your meal?" the chaplain said coming to sit down across the table from John.

"Are you here to pray for my soul or to find out my name?" John asked.

"Merely to sit with until it is time," the chaplain answered, "As I always do with inmates that are waiting for execution."

"I have no more interest in talking to you as I have any other time that you have come to see me," John said.

"Then we can just sit here in quiet while we wait," the chaplain said.

Two days after...

The detective joined the lawyer, who was standing in the cemetery looking at John's gravestone. The two men stood without speaking. There were a flock of song birds in a tree to their left and somewhere out of sight there was a lawn mower in use. The sun was warn enough to keep the fall chill away.

"Your office told me where to find you," the detective said.

"Another case?" the lawyer asked.

"No, I just wondered if you had figured out who he was." The detective gestured towards the gravestone. "I can't imagine how his wife feels. He went to work one morning and hasn't come home yet."

"Any missing person report?" the lawyer asked.

"None matching his description," the detective answered, "I check every time a new one comes in, just in case."

"She must know something about who he was," the lawyer said, "If I went missing my wife would have a bulletin out within a couple of hours."

"My ex would have put out a bulletin to let the world know that I had been arrested," the detective said.

The men were quiet again. The mower had stopped, but the birds were still chirping. A burst of wind tugged at their jackets and rearranged the leaves. It went passed and was gone.

"I thought he would fight longer." the detective said, "It was almost like he gave up the minute he was arrested and yet there was this air that said that no one could touch him. I thought he would come up with some evidence that would create at least reasonable doubt with the jury."

"He didn't have anything to refute any of the evidence." the lawyer said, "Then the prosecution had the video and I knew we had lost any rapport we had with the jury. The video was pretty damning."

"We were lucky to get it," the detective said, "Twenty minutes later and we would not have gotten it. But you could have appealed the death penalty."

"He called it a waste of time," the lawyer replied, "He didn't see any point in it, despite what I said. For someone who was not ready to die, he was willing to be killed. Did you ever figure out who Jane Doe was?"

"The woman's name was Sheryl Kinsley. Her mother came forward after we put out the picture of what she might have looked like," the detective answered, "Apparently they had a fight and had not been talking to each other so she didn't know her daughter was missing. Now she is dealing with the guilt of not being there for her daughter. I don't think it would have made any difference, aside from knowing that her daughter had died in the most horrible manner several years earlier. I'm not sure which is worse."

"I think all the women that came into John's life became a victim to him." the lawyer said, "His wife may have no idea what happened to him. Sheryl was killed by him. Melissa thought she could blackmail him and was killed instead. Then there are any number of women, who he had affairs with. That makes a lot of victims."

"And yet I can't feel sympathy for most of them," the detective said, "Each one chose to become his victim. Although he did succeed at one thing that may or may not be a good thing."

"What is that?" the lawyer asked.

"His wife will never be bothered by law enforcement," the detective said, "or anyone else."

"True," the lawyer said.

"Come on, I'll buy you a coffee before we both have to get back to work," the detective said as he started to turn away from the gravestone.

"Sure," the lawyer said. He didn't turn. The detective waited for him. The birds had flown off with the gust of wind, but the mower could be heard again.

"I still wonder who he was," the lawyer said before turning.

The Best Brownie Recipe

AN UNWANTED JOURNEY

Charles merely considered himself a big man. Most people considered him to be obese and right at this particular moment he agreed with them. Charles looked again at the meadow covered in the six-feet of snow as measured by the willow bushes around the edges. Then he looked down at the flimsy branches and thin strips of leather that made up the snowshoes Smith had given him. Charles wasn't sure they would hold him up in the snow, but he didn't have any choice. He had to get help or Smith would die.

Having no choice, Charles took his first few steps into field. His stomach had become a heavy weight on his mind as well as his middle. He expected the snow to give out beneath him and to be lost until spring. His steps were tentative and every crunch of snow caused him anxiety. However, the snowshoes held him on top of the snow and he didn't sink in over his head.

With some confidence, Charles quicken his pace. Every crunch still made him nervous about the snow collapsing under him, but every time nothing happened Charles felt like maybe he would make it.

Charles reached the other end of the meadow. This was

how far he would walk on a normal day if he got stuck on his writing, but today he couldn't turn around and wander back. He stopped briefly to catch his breath before continuing on.

The snow drifts and mounds and hills might as well have been flat ground until Charles stumbled upon them. It was all uniform brightness and the sunlight gave no sense of shadows anywhere. Even with the trees didn't help differentiate between the flat and the snow piles. The shoes didn't help much when Charles pushed them into the snow hills rather than walking on top of them.

Charles was going to have to thank Smith for making the snowshoes that not the week before he had scoffed at and wondered whatever he would use them for. He never planned to go walking while it was winter. In fact he had all intentions of stayed inside during all cold weather. And if Smith hadn't gotten sick, Charles would still be sitting by the fire trying to keep his ink thawed out enough to write with it.

But Smith had taken sick late yesterday and had been much worse this morning. From everything Charles had seen, it was likely that Smith wouldn't survive without medical help. The closest help was a town where Smith got their supplies and took Smith several days to get there and back. Charles knew which direction he was supposed to go, but not exactly how long it would take him to arrive. Then there was getting the people back who could help Smith.

This was hardly the activity Charles had planned for this winter. His agent was hounding him for his next novel, but Charles found himself unable to concentrate in the city. There was always another distraction; another dinner party, another book signing, another afternoon visit with friends. So, his agent found him some place without distractions. Charles had not realized how far from distractions it would be until he met Smith.

Smith lived in the back country with the closest

civilization being a small village a couple days walk because Smith did not own any modes of transportation aside from snowshoes. Charles had to hire a wagon and a team of horses to get his belongings to Smith's cabin. Smith's cabin was large enough that Charles had his own space without being in Smith's way.

So far, Charles had gotten along well with Smith for how little they talked. Smith seemed to like it that way. Charles had gotten a lot of work down on his novel as there was nothing out here to distract him. Then winter showed up and there was nothing else for him to do, except write.

Charles stopped and rested his hands on his knees. He really wanted to sit down and truly rest, but there was only snow to sit on. Charles felt that then he would have a wet back end and the cold would seep through the rest of his body. At the moment, he was not cold. Instead the sweat was soaking through his clothes and dripping off his face. He had never walked for a long or as far as he had just done. It had been morning when he had started out and now it was late afternoon.

The sun was headed for the horizon, which was the only change in the landscape as the snow was still the same as before and the amount of trees had not changed since he had left the field near Smith's cabin. If it wasn't for the footprints stretching behind him, Charles could have sworn he wasn't making any progress.

Charles dug into his bag and took out a piece of jerky. He was starving, but knew that he had very limited supplies There had been little he could take from the cabin. Charles did not know how much he would need to survive. This was already far less than he was used to eating, but he had such days before and as long as he ate a little Charles believed he could keep going.

The wind picked up as the sun disappeared behind the trees. Charles felt the sweat freeze rather than drip, which caused him to start shivering. He straightened up and went back to moving forward. Despite the tiredness that was starting to drag him down, Charles picked up his feet and continued his very much unwanted journey.

The novel was about a group of men trying to survive after being stranded away from civilization. Charles had thought he knew what a person might go through if they were stuck in such situations. Now he knew he had to go back and rewrite parts of his novel as there were a few facts he got wrong. The pieces needing work would not change the outcome very much and with the limited distractions he would have the changes done in no time. Charles worked to take his mind off the cold and tiredness by thinking about the novel.

The sun disappeared and Charles found himself dodging around trees he had been able to see earlier. It brought him out of the story and forced him to concentrate on his path. Occasionally Charles found himself stumbling over depressions in the snow that he might have noticed in the light. He tried not to let it slow him down, but he wished he had thought to bring a lantern as he avoided another tree.

Charles was not sure how long he had been stumbling in the dark when he had to stop to rest again. The dodging trees was adding time and expending more of his energy. But again he didn't want to sit, so he just stood still. He took out another piece of jerky to eat as he looked around. There was a thin slice of moon visible through the branches along with some stars. Neither helped to see the path through the snow and trees.

After finishing off the meat, Charles prepared himself to go on. He felt like curling up in a ball and going to sleep, but there was no bed or blanket around to tempt him. Charles looked in the direction he was heading and realized there was a glow on the horizon. It could only be lights from the village. That meant he must have been getting closer. Charles used that thought to bring a burst of energy.

Charles felt like he really could not go on any longer. He

was freezing, his boots were too heavy for him especially with the addition of the snow shoes, his fingers were numb, and his exhaustion was thorough. The night was deep and dark, but there was a glow on the horizon. He told himself that all he had to do was get to that glow and then he could rest. Smith needed him. His knees weren't sure they could actually make it, but he kept placing one foot in front of the other. A little farther. A little farther. A little farther.

With heavy eyelids, Charles missed the dip in the snow and stumbled. He fell to the ground was a groan. He wanted to get up, but the numbness of his right leg was marred by pain around his ankle. With strength he did not know he possessed, Charles picked himself up and struggled on. However, Charles only made it five more steps before his ankle gave out and he was left lying in the snow. He tried to keep his eyes open or call for help, but the frost had gotten the better of him.

Charles blinked and the light from the distance seemed to grow brighter. He first thought that the town got closer to him, but he finally determined that it was the light from heaven. When it reached him, he would be engulfed and then he wouldn't be so cold anymore.

The sound of yelling brought Charles close to consciousness, but he had trouble opening his eyes or moving around. He wanted to tell someone about Smith, but his tongue must have been frozen. Charles also felt like sinking back into the darkness because it was warmer there and it didn't feel like he was lying on hard snow.

"Sleds are here, Bert," a voice called.

"Good," a voice responded, "The biggest one is needed here and the smaller one needs to go to Smith's cabin."

"Why the Smith cabin?" someone nearby asked.

"Because if this gentleman came all the way from there, something has happened to Smith," the voice answered. He sounded like he was in charge and he sounded like he knew what he was doing. Charles hoped everything was as it sounded because there did not seem to be any way for him to telling the people what was going on. If fact, it seemed that Charles was not going to stay conscious for much longer.

Charles woke up to find himself lying on an army cot in a small white room. His ankle hurt, but he was warm with a wool blanket tucked in around him. There was the slight smell of antiseptic. All the light in the room came through a curtain, which was across the only window. It must have been mid-afternoon. Charles looked toward the door and found another army cot. Lying on it was Smith. Smith was asleep and beneath the wool blanket Charles could see a bandage peeking out. His face looked much better as well. Charles smiled to himself before snuggling down in the warmth and closing his eyes.

The Best Brownie Recipe

NOTES

The sailor referred to in this story has his own book, which is a collection of stories about his adventures.

A SAILOR APPEARED WITH A REQUEST

This day I was sitting in my library reading. It was a medium sized library, but lacked any windows for staring out of, which was why I was reading. It was a fascinating read about doctor who got himself in trouble with the English crown for treating a rebel, which caused him to be sold into slavery. Right now he was plotting the escape pf himself and the men who had been arrested with him from the plantation owner.

The stench of stale rum assaulted my nose causing me to look up from my book. There was a man sitting in the chair across from me. He was dressed in the uniform of a British Naval Captain from the 1600s, though his uniform was in need of a good laundering and he hadn't been updated on the need for personal hygiene. I placed the bookmark in my place before closing the book. This seemed like a bookmark type of interruption.

"Who are you and what are you doing in my library?" I asked him.

"I need you to write my story," he replied.

"You are drunk," I said.

"I still need you to write my story," he said.

"And who are you that I should write your story?" I asked.

"I am Captain Ashmore Dooley," he answered.

"I don't remember ever hearing about you," I replied as I prepared to go back at my book.

"That is why I need you to write my story," he said, "So people know who I am and what I did."

"And what did you do?" I asked without looking up.

"I went on adventures," he replied.

"And?" I asked.

"It was for the English king," he said.

"Unless I'm mistaken, you're Irish." I lowered my book a little to look at him.

"I am," Captain Dooley said, "Which is why you need to write my story."

"I am still not sure how it is unique enough to write your story," I replied as I brought my book up to focused on it.

"Let me tell you one," Captain Dooley said. I looked up at him from my book.

"It was the Thursday after we passed Spain..."

My book ended up in my lap, forgotten for the moment as I listened.

"Cathal saluted and went to pass along the order."

My fingers itched as Captain Dooley finished his story. I picked up the notebook from the table beside my chair. Taking the pen out of the coil, I clicked the end and started writing. I became unaware of everything except the page, my pen, and the smell of stale rum.

When I finally looked up from my notebook, Captain Dooley was not there. He left behind the smell and several story ideas. I gathered the story ideas up and put them down in the notebook. Setting down the book I had been reading, I giggled as I started writing again.

It was the Tuesday after the storm blew us off course...

The Best Brownie Recipe

A WEIGHT PROBLEM

Jennifer stepped outside into the morning cold only far enough to pick up the paper from where the newspaper delivery person had dropped it on her doorstep. She closed and locked the door behind her. It was a good day to stay inside, but then Jennifer knew that every day was a good day to stay inside when you were her size. Jennifer looked at the headline as she trudged up the stairs to the main floor. Candy store bust, was what it read. Then it went on about how many kilograms of chocolate bars and other candies the police took from a house across town from the neighbourhood where Jennifer lived. There were four people under arrest for selling an illegal substance.

Jennifer dropped the paper on to the table. She went into her kitchen and stirred the scrambled eggs and peppers that were cooking in the pan. Then she poured herself a glass of orange juice before sitting down in the chair. She turned to the second page of the paper. The headline was about a starlet being placed in court ordered weight camp. Jennifer shivered at the memories of the court ordered weight camps. She had seen too many of them. Of course, the starlet would be at ones different from the one she experienced, but that did not change the horror of what they were.

Jennifer had been sent too many camps because she weighed more than the height weight charts said she should be. Every time they put her on a strict diet along with a torturous amount of exercise. She lived through the set amount of time she could be kept at the camp, but she was never exactly what society expected she should be. Now she did not dare let anyone see her because she would be sent back to the pain and the terror.

The first camp Jennifer had gone voluntarily because she thought it would change her into what was expected of her. Her parents had seen her balloon out after puberty and the trouble it caused at school. She was the kid the gym teachers made run extra laps. The other kids had taken to calling her candy store, which the teachers never did anything about because they thought it would encourage her to lose the weight. Everyone was happy to hear that she had gone to the camp, but when she had not lost all of the excess weight the taunting returned.

Jennifer knew her parents were ashamed of her. They never asked her to go out with them and her brother. As far as she could tell, they never mentioned her to anyone, unless the person knew enough to ask. They sent cards of support when they heard she had been sent back to one of the camps. The cards just said they believed that she could lose the weight this time.

The starlet staring up from the front page of the paper was too thin from having too busy a schedule and not enough time to take care of herself. Jennifer felt pity for the girl. No one deserved to be placed in that situation, but the lawmakers and enforcers believed they were doing people a favour. Everyone should be the correct weight for their height according to the chart. Junk food was outlawed and nutritionists examined people's groceries at the checkout to make sure they were getting the proper amount of vitamins and minerals necessary.

Jennifer had taken to ordering her groceries online so she would not have to leave her apartment. The delivery boy was willing to leave the food on the step and take the envelope out of the mail box. He probably did the same for others in similar situations as Jennifer. She had tried to go shopping, but everyone always looked at her as if she was stuffing her cart full of junk food and whispering about why someone of her weight was let out of a camp if she was not the weight she was supposed to be. Also she had only been able to find work online because no one was willing hire a fat person.

Jennifer closed the paper and threw it into the recycling container. She did not want to read more about the world from her position of observer. Instead she got up and went to the window. She peered out the small opening in her curtains and down at the sidewalk below. The other people in the neighbouring apartments were heading out on their mandatory morning runs. Even if the government officials did not demand they do it, medical insurance companies were no longer willing to cover anyone who did not exercise daily.

Jennifer sighed. Sometimes she would lose the weight, but only when they restricted her diet to the point of starvation and exercised her to exhaustion. But always she would get home and as soon as she started eating normally she was right back where she started. It was better if Jennifer did not go and be seen. If she was seen, she would be reported and everything would start all over again. She was tired of that.

Jennifer knew that she could have a normal life. She could go out running with everyone else. She could have a job with medical insurance and health benefits. She could go into any store and never be forced to leave because people were staring at her. She could stand on her porch and enjoy the sunlight. Her parents would invite her to things and would no longer feel shame at the very thought of her. She might even find someone to date or have her own family. If only she were not overweight. If only she was the hundred and forty-four pounds the chart said she should be.

Jennifer had wished for all that. She wished she never had to be in another camp ever again. She wished she could talk with other people in person and get to know them. She wished they would not call the enforcers to her door. She wished her build did not attract the extra pounds. She wished she had been born in a different time period when being overweight was a good thing. But most of all, Jennifer wished for the fifteen pounds to go away.

NOTES

I wrote Mer Island for a contest. It was through Okanagan College and it involved being given three hours to write a story. As usual with contests I did not win, but I think the story turned out well. It did not take me three hours to write it.

MER ISLAND

My name is Merida, but my friends call me Mer. And right now I'm fast coming to the conclusion that I was not dead. It is a surprise since I had been swallowing water while the ship had sunk around me. Not only was I alive, but I was lying in sand. Sand that was creeping into places it shouldn't be despite the fact that I hadn't moved. The lack of comfort in my position caused me to open my eyes. My eyelids parted slowly as the grit let go.

There was dark blue sky above me as if it was late evening. The sun was off to my left. I could also see tree branches further from the water. I sat up with a certain amount of care. My head swam for a moment, but otherwise I seemed to be okay. I was sitting on a wide expanse of beach that eventually curved towards each other. It was either a piece of land jutting out or an island. Based on where the ship was when I sank, this was probably an island. Mostly likely uncharted, so I couldn't expect rescue coming any time soon.

I stood up and dusted the dry sand off the front of my dress. I did the best that I could about the wet sand on my back, but there was little progress there. The trees were far enough apart that I could see several rows in. It was also thick enough I didn't want to explore too far if night was going to fall soon. Instead I gathered fallen branches and tuffs of dried grass, which I used to prepare an area on the beach for a fire.

My brother had been a survivalist. He had spent so much time in our back yard making fires and eating squirrel he had killed himself. It had unnerved the neighbourhood, but my parents had made him promise not to eat any pets. Sometimes he appreciated the evenings I would go out there with the stolen bag of marshmallows for us to roast. So, starting this fire was simple. Unfortunately, my brother wasn't there to kill anything for me to eat and the pantry with the marshmallows was a long way away.

Conscription had gotten my brother and my parents were fighting for their health. That was why I agreed to be shipped away to some South American country as a nanny for a rich American family. It was supposed to be far enough from the war that I would be safe as well as making some money I could send home to help my family. And then the ship I had passage on sunk leaving me alone on this beach.

My thoughts, as I stared into the flames I was using for warmth, were interrupted by the sound of someone walking along the sand. I looked in that direction, but at first I could not see anything due to my eyes being washed out by the light. As they got used to the dark, I could see the figure coming towards me. He didn't look like he had washed up from the same ship I had. In fact, he looked like he had washed up a long time ago. His clothes were dirty and ripped. His beard and hair quite long. He was also barefoot. It was difficult to see his face in the limited light, especially with most of it hidden with hair. He stopped on the other side of the fire.

"Under the weather?" he asked.

"Washed up," I replied.

"It is going to rain tonight," he said.

"I don't see any clouds for it to come from," I said.

"The weather comes in fast," he said, "One minute you are enjoying the sunshine and the next you're in a typhoon."

"Must be hard on the wild life," I said.

"Doesn't bother the fish at all," he said, "But it'll bother you and me."

"You have survived it," I said.

"I have shelter," he said, "And I am willing to share."

"That is very nice of you," I said.

"Company doesn't come around here very often," he said.

"I am surprised it comes around at all," I said.

"They never stay long," he said, "Always in a hurry to leave."

"Have you seen any other survivors on this island from the ship I was on?" I asked.

"No," he said, "Only you."

"How far is your shelter?" I asked.

"A short way," he said as he pointed into the trees,

"I suppose I have nowhere else to go," I said.

He looked back at me, but didn't response to me statement. The fire had not been big due to me not finding large pieces to burn and since I had not fed it more, it was burning down. I wasn't not sure about the man but I had little choice. I got to my feet. More sand came off when I brushed my backside this time because it had time to dry. There was still a lot still stuck though.

The man led the way into the trees. With the sun having gone down, it was hard to keep him in sight but I managed. He had the path memorized while I tripped over roots and rocks. He kept his distance instead of offering to assist me as if he knew I didn't want his help.

He was right about how far it was to his shelter. It had only been a short walk before we came to a cave with a door made from boat scraps. It may have kept out anything large, but it looked like it may collapse if slammed. The man held it open for me.

Inside, the cave was lit with two clay bowls filled with something that burned like candles. There was a crude table with a chair as well as dried grass piled into the form of a bed. I couldn't see much further into the back of the cave, but there was some clutter at the base of the walls.

"Welcome to my humble shelter," the man said, "Bathroom facilities are outside to the right and the kitchen is outside to the left."

I missed my fire, but it was warmer than sitting on the beach. I sat down a little father into the cave than the pile of bed and rested against the stone. There was something beside my hand. I picked it up without really thinking. The white gleamed in the candle light as I looked at the bone in my hand.

"Pig," the man said as he sat down on the bed, "Wild pigs used to live on this island." He didn't say anything else before blowing out the candles and making himself comfortable in the bed. I put the bone back in the floor and wrapped my arms around my knees to make myself as small as possible. I knew the bone had been from someone's hand and pigs didn't have those. Sleep was elusive.

I woke to sounds of someone moving around outside. Once again I was surprised that I wasn't dead. There was light coming in the open door as if the sun was peaking in its quest westward. I got to my feet and walked to the entrance of the cave. It looked like a beautiful day, but there was a hint that it had rained at some point during the night. The man was sitting on a rock working on a hunting spear. He seemed to be deeply engaged in his work as he didn't notice me. I stepped out of the cave and went to the right.

The man didn't try to stop me from going anywhere and doing anything. And once I had spent time exploring the island, I understood why. There was nowhere I could go. It was a small island in the middle of a large ocean, which was unlikely to be on any trade routes. The ship I had been traveling on was only nearby because a storm had blown us off course. All there was around was trees and a man who had been here much too long.

I found a spot as far away from the man's shelter and obvious hunting trails. I was careful as I built myself an area hidden by brush and anything else I could use as camouflage. It took me most of the day to get it finished to my specifications and I found myself very hungry by the time I was done. The man had said there was only fish to eat and having seen no animals all day I believed him. But I didn't have anything with which to fish.

Using his hunting trails, I found my way back to his shelter. He was sitting beside a fire on the left side of the cave. He was using clay made into a grill to cook some fish over the fire. It smelled delicious.

"I thought you might be back," he said, "So I caught one extra."

"Thank you," I said sitting down on a nearby rock.

"Found a place out from under the weather?" the man asked.

"Somewhat," I answered, "It is still in progress, but I should have a roof on it soon."

"You are welcome to share my cave anytime you need," he said. He dished up the fish on to clay plates. He handed one to me.

"Thank you," I said taking the plate.

"Enjoy," the man said with a smile. He lacked several teeth along the right side and the rest looked in need of some care.

"How did you end up here?" I asked as I carefully pulled apart the fish with my fingers. It was hot.

"The captain suspected me of stealing," he said, "Figured this was a good a punishment as any."

"Did you steal something?" I asked.

"No," he answered, but didn't provide any further details. My instincts suggested that his explanation was a lie, but I wasn't sure I wanted to hear the truth from him. There was no further conversation as we ate.

When supper was finished I cleaned the plate in the water he had for that purpose. Then I wandered back to my hiding spot. I was careful about being followed, but figured that he really wouldn't bother. This island wasn't big and he knew it well. I just hoped he wouldn't know it that well.

I got back to my space just as the sun was on the horizon. It kept my area lit until it was gone for the day. Then it was dark until the moon rose to provide me with its light. I had laid down to sleep when the sun left, but with the moon light I found myself unable to sleep. Finally, I gave up and started working on my project. Only when exhaustion got its grip on me did I fall asleep.

I am not quite sure how much time passed as each day was similar to the last one. Even when I am near a calendar I can lose track of days. I made progress on my project and the man said and did nothing to make me nervous. Of course, that made me worry. The only difference in his behaviour was his lack of interest in the fish he cooked every night. At first was merely lengthening of the time he took to eat it, but now he is not even finishing the pieces on his plate. His face seemed to be narrowing as if he was not eating at all, except for that piece of fish. Unfortunately, my project was not ready to be put to use.

Then the storm appeared on the horizon. I guess a more accurate description would be that it built up over several days and appeared to be closer to the typhoon the man had talked about rather than a nice thunder storm like I enjoyed back home. But this particular day, it was closing over head.

I left my project to join the man for supper as usual. He was sitting by the fire with the fish grilling, as if it was a usual day. But there was something wrong. His face had taken on a sinister quality and his eyes studied me under his bushy eyebrows as if he was trying to decide which part would taste the best. He served me the fish as if there was nothing wrong. I tried not to appear watchful as I ate.

"Still under the weather?" he asked as I was washing the clay plate.

"I managed to build the roof," I answered, "Though I am not sure how well it will hold up if the storm hits."

"I would suggest you move into my cave until the storm passes," he said, "These storms are nothing like those you get inland. The rain alone has been known to take down trees. The cave is the best shelter around."

Something in my gut told me to run and the flickering light in the man's eyes suggested the same.

"I have to go gather my stuff first," I said as I backed away from him. As much as I was trying to keep myself calm, he realized that I wasn't. He reached down the grab the hunting spear, but I didn't stick around to see anything else. I turned and ran.

The days on this island had helped me to know the paths. This prevented me from tripping on roots and helped me avoid rocks. I would have been dead for sure without that knowledge. The man may not have been running after me, but I could hear his pursuit. He knew these paths better than I did.

Knowing my chances were slim in the areas he had already claimed I headed into the trees and off the path. I went until I was sure he could not see me. Then I climbed the thickest tree in the group. I went up as far as I could. Once I was settled on the branch, I looked down. The man was coming through the trees and looking for signs of my passage. I had left far too many. My brother would have been disappointed in me.

The man finally reached the area where all traces of me disappeared. He searched the ground for tracks. I knew my time was limited if I wanted to remain alive. Near me was a branch that was half broken off and did not take much to pull it off completely. It was heavy enough to do damage. I waited until the man was under me before I dropped it. Luck was with me in that moment because it hit the man in the head. He collapsed. I waited for a moment to see if he would move, but he didn't.

I climbed down the tree. Once on the ground, I headed away from him. I couldn't tell whether I had killed him or not, but if not I didn't have much time. I ran through the trees back to my hiding spot. Just as I arrived the rain started. It may not have been enough to damage trees, but it was cold and I was soaked in seconds. The pit I had dug for my work area was saturated in mere minutes. The raft was only three logs in size as it had been difficult to move each one and prepare them to be lashed together, but it was enough to float me away from this island. That was all I needed it to do.

The pit was turning into a swimming pool as I worked to push the raft out. The mud was slippery and my strength was limited. The adrenaline coursing through my body helped, but it still took much too long to get the raft on to the grass at the edge of the pit. The grass was also slick with the rain, but this helped move it rather than slow me down further. At a much faster speed I got the raft to the edge of the trees. The beach was the only standing between me and the ocean. It was a large area without any terrain useful for hiding. Any dips in the sand were full with water and the rain prevented me from seeing very far down the beach.

I checked as carefully as I could before I moved out from the trees. I pulled the raft for all that I was worth. The sand slowed my progress as much as the rain. I could see very little, except when the lightning made the whole situation worse. I had gotten the raft to the edge of the water and was moving around it to push it the rest of the way when I saw the silhouette lit up by the flash in the sky. I was not going to make it. Even if I got the raft into the water, I would not be able to get far enough away before he reached me.

Instead I turned towards him and braced myself. The only thing I had was my brother's hunting knife, which he had given to me before the army had abducted him. I removed it from its hiding place under my sleeve. Then I dodged the hunting spear the man threw at him. Wit the rain beating down his accuracy was off and I was able to avoid it.

Then he charged at me. I couldn't tell whether he had another weapon. I waited until he was just about to me to sidestep away from him. He stopped his charge and turned to me. With his hands reaching out for me, I slashed at them with the knife. He pulled back when he felt the metal go through his right hand. I backed off from him. He noticed and came at me again. This time he tried to grab for my wrist. I was a second quicker and went to the right, but I slipped in a pool of water and went down. He reached out for me. I rolled away from him. He continued to chase me. I got to my feet as he was close to me. He was trying to grab me and wasn't expecting me to be so close. I pushed the knife into his stomach and pulled up. It ripped through much of his flesh before I pulled it out. He froze in shock.

I didn't stick around to see how much damage I had done. Instead I went back to the raft and pushed it into the water with all my remaining strength. Once it was floating, I continued to push it until I could no longer reach bottom and still be able to get on. The one paddle I have managed to make was not as long as I wanted, but I managed to use it to push the rafter a little further. Finally, the waves took over in pushing the raft away from the island. I used the paddle to help.

Only when I was sure about the distance, did I look back. I could barely make out anything through the rain, but I could have sworn the man was standing there on the beach cursing at me. I turned back around and put as much distance between me and that island as I could.

The Best Brownie Recipe

B. Heather Mantler

MRS. JONES

Mrs. Jones was the fastest knitter west of the Rocky Mountains. She could knit toques in mere minutes and sweaters in half an hour. Despite her attempts from the day after she retired, her yarn collection hardly looked like it had been touched. It was all packed in to the room, which had one point been one of the children's rooms, and there was still more yarn than space.

Lately the weather had turned back and Mrs. Jones had plenty of time to knit as she could not get out to do any errands or go visit friends. So, she had spent the time getting her sweaters down to twenty minutes and then fifteen. Now she could do them less than five.

Overnight it had snowed plenty and this morning when Mrs. Jones got up there was a deep fog surrounding her house. Something about it felt wrong and Mrs. Jones felt a shiver go up her spine that had nothing to do with the cold. She pulled on her warmest parka and stuck her feet into her boots. Then she stepped outside and peering into the post-dawn light. At first, Mrs. Jones could see nothing to be concerned over. Then she saw the movement. It was difficult to discern due to the objects moving being the same paleness of the fog and snow, but then Mrs. Jones realized what they were.

Mrs. Jones rushed inside and picked up the phone. She sighed with relief as the line had not been cut. Then she dialed the number for her son, the fire chef.

"Hello," his voice is rough with sleep.

"They are here," Mrs. Jones breathing out the sentence.

"Are you sure?" her son was instantly alert.

"I know what I saw," Mrs. Jones said, "They are here."

"Wait someplace safe," her son said, "I'll get there as fast as I can."

Mrs. Jones hung up. She looked out the window again. The movement was no longer dim shapes in the fog, but the snowmen marching forward. Mrs. Jones looked around for any weapon she could find, but the only thing she saw were her knitting needles. She grabbed them up and her basket of yarn. Going outside, she sat on the porch and started knitting.

The first snowman was knitted up in the cutest sweater before he knew what was happening. Those sweaters of Mrs. Jones were meant to keep a person warm in the coldest of conditions. He melted quickly in that warmth. Mrs. Jones had the next sweater done before he was finished turning into a frozen puddle.

Mrs. Jones kept going until her son and the other firemen showed up with their steam hose and was able to take care of the rest.

The Best Brownie Recipe

NOTES

The Lake is another story I wrote for a contest. I made a mistake. After I finished writing the story, I realized I had too many words and I started to edit down to the word count for the contest. My mistake was to edit without saving a copy of the original version. Always save the original version and save the edited version as a separate file.

THE LAKE

"Mom, look what I can do!"

"Dad, make her stop splashing me!"

"Stacey, don't swim that far out!"

"Mark, quit throwing sand!"

"Honey, the fire is just right for cooking the hot dogs."

Stacey flipped the page of the photo album. The card in the top slot gave the year in her mother's perfect handwriting. The pictures were similar to the last ones. Lake Leechwood was the same shade of blue and the sand the same of off-white. Mark was a foot taller than the last pictures and Stacey's own bathing suit was a different colour.

Stacey flipped through that year and the next several years of trips to the lake. Finally she came to the very last photograph. It was Lake Leechwood as it always looked as they packed up their stuff to go home. It was empty and peaceful. The oranges and pinks of the sunset that rose above the pine trees reflected in parts of the water. Stacey remembered her and Mark never wanting to leave.. When she was ten Stacey had wanted to preserve that lake until the next year when they would be back, so she had used her father's camera to take this picture. A copy had been attached to her mirror all winter. But the next year they hadn't gone back to Lake Leechwood. No, they had gone to a pool because it was closer. They had never gone back to the lake.

The sound of the front door opening brought Stacey back to the present. Stacey heard the door close and then Perry came into the living room.

"Hi," Perry said, "How was your day?" He bent down to kiss her.

"It was good," Stacey answered.

"What is that?" Perry gestured toward the photo album.

"My mother was going through the basement trying to figure out how to reduce the amount of stuff they have before they move into the seniors complex," Stacey answered, "She sent me a box full of stuff. This is a photo album of all the trips we took to Lake Leechwood."

"Must have been quite a few," Perry picked up the album to flip through it.

"Every year until I turned eleven," Stacey said.

"It looks like you had fun," Perry said.

"It was lots of fun," Stacey said, "Didn't you ever go to the lake when you were a kid?"

"No," Perry said, "We had pool in our backyard, why go anywhere when you can swim at home for free?"

"I guess that makes sense, though it isn't half as much fun," Stacey said, "The coldness of the water, the making friends with strangers, and trying to clean sand off your feet so that you can put your shoes on to go home."

"So, why did you stop going when you were eleven," Perry asked.

"I don't know," Stacey answered, "My parents started taking us to the public swimming pool instead of the lake. They gave excuses why, but never really gave a good reason."

"Things change," Perry said.

"I know," Stacey said.

At the restaurant where they had supper the hostess seated them and the waiter brought out their choice of wine. And their order had been taken.

"So, have you decided where we are going during our two-week vacation?" Perry asked, "Since it is your turn to choose the place."

"Not yet," Stacey answered, "I will figure it out by Friday night, don't worry."

"I trust you," Perry said.

The next day Stacey came home from work after lunch. She changed into jeans and a t-shirt before starting to clean up the house starting with the kitchen. When she got to the living room she found her mother's box still sitting on the coffee table. Slowly she went through each piece and found it a place on a shelf or wrapped back up and placed in a shoebox. After Stacey tossed the box in the recycling she noticed the album still sitting on the couch. She picked it up and opened it to the last page. The last photograph drew her in as if it was calling to her. An idea came to Stacey making her smile. She closed the album and carefully placed it on the shelf with the rest of the photo albums. Then she went on with her cleaning.

When Perry arrived home after work she had finished cleaning the house and had supper ready. They sat down to eat.

"I had an idea about our vacation," Stacey said.

"What is it?" Perry asked.

"I want to see if we can find Lake Leechwood," Stacey answered.

"Are you sure?" Perry asked.

"I want to see it again," Stacey answered, "And you need to see how much fun it is to go to a lake for a day."

"And what are we going to do once we have found it?"

Perry asked.

"Spend the rest of the time reading those piles of books we keep saying we will read," Stacey answered, "That is what a vacation is for, isn't it?"

"I suppose it is," Perry said, "What is it going to take to find this lake?"

"Research," Stacey answered, "I know that name, but I can never remember how we got out there. I will start that tomorrow after work."

"Okay," Perry said.

Friday after work Stacey arrived home excited about the job of finding Lake Leechwood. She sat down at her laptop and got started.

Two hours later, when she gave up the search to make supper, Stacey had not found any website that would tell her where Lake Leechwood was. She found a variety of lakes that offered camping or cabins, a children's camp, and a website that gave all the gory details about leeches. The excitement was replaced by frustration until Stacey decided that this project would not be as much fun if it was easy.

The next day Stacey went to the tourist information centre and picked up a map of the area. There was a list of nearby lakes that she took with her. At home Stacey laid the map out on the dining room table. She figured out what distance it would be if it took two hours to travel there from the house her parents used to own and made a circle on the map. Then she made a list of all the lakes in that area.

That evening while Perry went and got the gas tank filled Stacey packed a lunch. They would set out the next morning for a place called Leech Lake. It sounded like the most likely of the whole list that she had.

After breakfast Perry and Stacey headed off with a packed up car and high hopes. Stacey sat back and enjoyed the trip while Perry drove.

Two hours down the road they came to a sign that said the turn off to Leech Lake was 500 metres ahead. Stacey sat up with excitement as Perry turned on to the road. It was ten minutes down a paved road to the parking lot. The parking lot was close to full. Perry took a space near the end far from the path down to the lake. There were too many trees to see the lake from the parking lot. The parking lot had the darker asphalt and bright lines of being new. Stacey got out of the car. Perry followed her example.

"Is this it?" Perry asked.

"I'm not sure," Stacey answered. Perry pushed the button on his remote and the doors clicked to say they were locked.

"Well, let's go down to the lake," Perry started towards the path. Stacey followed him. The path was two-foot wide, gravelled space between trees. It twisted a few times before straightening out at an area of picnic tables. The tables were several feet apart and none of them had the fire pits Stacey remembered. From here the path was sand. Perry and Stacey followed it down. Once clear of the trees the lake stretched out before them. It was a muddy blue with dots of people in boats all over it. The beach was full of families enjoying a day at the lake. Stacey had stopped to take it all in. A beach ball landed at her feet. Stacey looked down at it. A small boy came up, but was hesitant to come too close and get his ball. Stacey smiled at him and he came close enough to get his ball before running off with it.

"Is this it?" Perry asked.

"No," Stacey answered, "It is a very nice lake, but it isn't the one we're looking for."

"How about we stay for lunch anyway?" Perry asked.

"Sure," Stacey said. Perry turned and went back up the path. Stacey watched the scene for a few more minutes before heading up the path. She went as far as the picnic tables. Finding one without anyone's belongings claiming it she sat down and waited for Perry.

Perry brought the lunch. After they ate Perry and Stacey drove back home. At home Stacey studied the map and her list. She finally decided on one that looked like it might be what they were looking for.

The next day they set out again. The lake was not Lake Leechwood. They ate lunch and went home.

This time Stacey made a list of ten more lakes and put them into the order that her and Perry would visit them. Then she packed a lunch for the next day.

The lake they went to this time had been turned into a sand pit. The parking lot still existed, but the picnic tables, change rooms, a jungle gym, and the lifeguard station had all been removed. The remains of these items were in one corner of the parking lot where they had been dumped. Through the stumps showing where the trees had been Stacey looked at the sand pit.

"Is this where it was?" Perry asked as they stared at it.

"No," Stacey answered, "There was no lifeguard station or jungle gym at Lake Leechwood."

"Good," Perry said, "I saw a rest stop back ways on the highway. Why don't we have lunch there?"

"Sure," Stacey said. They got back into the car and drove away. Stacey looked at the lake until it disappeared from sight. She told herself that challenges weren't fun it they were easy. They stopped for lunch before heading home.

As the week wore on they went to a different lake every day. The stuff they were taking with them in case they found the lake had taken up residence just inside the front door because it was easier than putting it all away just to take it out again.

Stacey was starting to feel drained by Friday, so she and Perry stayed at home on Saturday. They both enjoyed reading in the shade on the back deck and going to a friend's barbeque for supper. Sunday they went back out looking for Lake Leechwood.

The lake they came to on Sunday was beautiful. The water sparkled blue with the sand a matching white. The change rooms had flushable toilets and all the picnic tables were covered. It definitely was not Lake Leechwood, but Perry and Stacey unpacked the car. They set up their lawn chairs in a nice spot and changed into swimwear. And they joined the other people having fun at the lake.

"You were right," Perry commented as they turned out of the parking lot and on to the highway to head home, "A day at the lake is fun."

"It was nice," Stacey said, "But I'm not sure why they had to create a lake just to have fun."

"What do you mean create a lake?" Perry asked.

"The lake was perfectly round," Stacey said, "And there was no plants or animal life in it. The temperature was perfect for swimming, not too cold. It felt man made. A real lake if it didn't occur naturally it is not there."

"Okay," Perry said, "It was fun anyway."

"Yes, it was still a good day at a lake," Stacey said.

Monday to Thursday they visited another four lakes, one each day. Thursday night Stacey went to bed with one more lake on her list, a packed lunch, and a sense of despair that they wouldn't find lake Leechwood. She stared at the ceiling for a long time before she finally fell asleep.

When Perry and Stacey woke up Friday morning they found it to be sunny and warm. They were sweating just packing everything out to the car for that final trip. Once inside, Perry turned on the air conditioner and they headed for the last lake on the list. The traffic was heavy and their pace was slowed. It took three hours to get to the lake. They arrived to a full parking lot and a lake that was not what they were looking for. After lunch they headed back.

The traffic was still heavy. They ended up stopping for supper at a place along the way.

"What are you folks doing up this way?" the man at the counter asked as they sat down.

"We're looking for a specific lake," Stacey told him.

"Which one?" the man asked.

"Lake Leechwood," Stacey answered.

"I remember that lake," the man said, "Its half an hour east of here."

Stacey also couldn't wait for supper to be over. Finally it was. She and Perry followed the man's directions. Stacey's excitement mounted as they found the sign for the turn off. It looked old and battered but you could see read it. The gravel road that led to the gravel parking lot had a lot of ruts and holes. Perry and Stacey were well shaken up by the time they parked in the empty lot. Stacey could see the change rooms from where they parked. The buildings looked like no one had tended them since Stacey had last been here. Stacey got out of the car. Perry followed her as she was just about running. The picnic tables in groups with covers over them, though a couple of the covers had crashed in.

'This is it!" Stacey called to Perry as she continued running. Finally she came around the last corned in the path that blocked her view of the lake. Stacey stopped. The sun was starting to going down, just like it had showed in the picture. But now it was disappearing behind a large factory, instead of trees. The blue water was now an inky grey and the sand was black where the water went over it. Stacey could even see chunks of stuff floating in the water. She heard Perry catch up to her and stop. They were silent as the sun was disappearing. In the last rays of light Stacey turned to head back to the car. The light reflected off the teardrop rolling down Stacey's face.

The Best Brownie Recipe

B. Heather Mantler

GIRLFRIEND TROUBLE

It was 2:00am on July 24th when Tony Powell woke from a deep sleep to find himself in need of rushing to the bathroom. Without thought or time wasted, Tony made it in time to avoid an accident. Since he was twenty-five, Tony believed that to be a good thing.

Tony sat there in a semi-wake state, his eyelids kept trying to close but the organs of elimination continued their purge. And continued their purge. Tony eyelids stayed open a little longer as his brain started to register the length of time he sat there. He blinked several more times as he woke up further. Tony wondered what he could have eaten which result in this situation.

Noise came through from the next apartment. It was a television show turned up too loud as men and women shouted at each other. Tony couldn't tell exactly what the argument was about, but the people were almost incoherent in their rage.

The flow was easing a bit and Tony started feeling relieved. He could go back to bed soon. Tony looked over at the toilet paper roll and found an empty roll with a piece of note paper taped to it. Without thought to the note paper,

Tony started searching under the sink for the package he had purchased the other day. He was sure it had to be there somewhere.

Wherever he had put the toilet paper, it was not in there. The slip of plastic from the bag was lying on under the sink, but the package was missing. Tony inched a little forward to keep searching, but found the need to move back in place. His organs of elimination were not finished yet.

Tony's attention went back to the piece of note paper. It had his name on it in his girlfriend's handwriting. He peeled it off the cardboard and opened the note up. Tony started reading.

Tony

I'm sure by now you realized I have taken all of your toilet paper and I thought I should tell why I'm dumping you. I saw you with the large chested blonde at Jake's restaurant the other day. I watched as she leaned over to talk to you and just about fell out of her top.

I took a couple days to think about the incident, but I did manage to figure out a suitable punishment for your crime. The chili I left in your fridge and you thought was so delicious had a special ingredient, half a bottle of laxatives.

Enjoy your single life without toilet paper.

Jewel

Tony reread the note as he tried to remember the large-chested blonde that he had gone out with in the last week or so. Tony did not remember such a person. He went through the note for a third time. This time he stopped on the phrase at Jake's restaurant. The last time he had been to Jake's restaurant for lunch was two weeks ago when his friend, Michael, was visiting. Michael's girlfriend had been with them for lunch. She had blonde streaks in her hair, but she was a brunette. Tony did remember her top having a low neckline, however he would not have classified her as large-chested.

All of which still left him sitting in the bathroom, lacking toilet paper, and with his phone on his bedside table. Tony threw the note in the garbage can before looking around for a substitute for the toilet paper that was not there. He did not see any item suitable. And Tony's phone was in the other room. He needed his phone to call someone who could bring him some toilet paper.

The shower dripped causing Tony to gaze up at it in awareness. He got off the porcelain basin before flushing and climbed into the bathtub. He used the shower to wash himself off. Once clean, Tony wrapped a towel around his waist and headed into the bedroom.

Tony picked his phone off the bedside table and started going through his contacts list. He did not get very far when the flow warning arrived. Tony rushed back to the bathroom, tossing the towel on the floor where his pajama pants lay. There was a sense of relief to have gotten to his seat on time.

The phone was in his hand and Tony stared at it thoughtful. The direness of his situation was sinking in. If he called any of his friends, they would taunt him about it for the rest of his life. Even his best friend would never let him forget calling up at two-thirty in the morning to ask about getting some toilet paper.

Tony thought about calling his mother, but hesitated. She would come to the rescue in an instant no matter the time or the emergency. But at such an early time of the morning, she should be a last resort, not the first call. He was an adult after all.

At that thought, Tony started scrolling through his contacts. There must be someone he could call at quarter to three who would bring him the material he was in most need of. Those who he counted as true friends taunted him from their photos. There were also family members in their grey-haired, false-teethed portraits of people who were only two hours from getting up and needed their rest.

Acquaintances were all that were left to choose from and none of them were close enough to call. Most would assume it was a crank call or their phones would vibrate without waking them. Tony was sure any of them who did answer probably would never accept calls from him again, if they didn't delete him completely from their phones.

A final name came up and Tony pressed to dial. The ringing coming through let him know Jewel hadn't turned off her phone. But it ended in a request to leave a voicemail. Tony tried again and received the same response.

Tony thought about trying again. And for a brief moment he was concerned about waking her. At that thought his thumb hit redial. Ringing and request. After the fifth attempt calling Tony gave up. Nothing was disturbing Jewel's sleep tonight.

Tony gave up and gave in. He didn't see any other options. The toilet paper was gone, friends couldn't be called, and Jewel was not picking up. Tony called his mom. The phone rand twice before it was picked up.

"Hello?" her voice was muffled with sleep.

"Mom, I need your help," Tony said.

"Is that Tony again?" his father's voice could be heard loud and clear from the other side of the bed.

"Quiet, Dear," Tony's mom covered the phone, "Tony, what is it?"

"He needs to get rid of that girlfriend of his before she completely cripples his emotional being," Tony's father said, "He can't keep calling you to deal with her."

"I ran out of toilet paper," Tony said, but he wanted to say he made a mistake and hang up.

"Thought you were going shopping yesterday," Tony's mom said.

"I forgot," Tony's voice turned whiny even as he tried for it not to.

"I'll be over as soon I can," Tony's mom said, "I've got

my key so you don't even have to get up."

"Thank you, Mom," Tony said before hanging up. He put his phone on the counter. Tony put his head in his hands. Not only had he lost his girlfriend, but he was going to have to buy more toilet paper tomorrow.

NOTES

This story (What Happened?) was inspired by the Dierks Bentley song Somewhere on a Beach. I had heard the song on the radio and it provided the idea for the story. I had written the story before I found the video on youtube.

WHAT HAPPENED?

Owen poured the whiskey into the glass and tried to remember if it was his third or fourth refill. Must be his third; he wasn't likely to still be counting at four. Though Owen couldn't quite be sure. The only thing he was sure of was that Hilary wouldn't be back into his life. Despite everything he had done to save the relationship, it was over. She was rid of him permanently; though she may not want to be when she realized she doesn't like being lonely. That was what happened last time, but back then he was okay getting back together with her. Now he was too tired of her behaviour.

Owen used the whiskey to wash down the bitterness before refilling the glass. The last one must have been the third one because he really didn't care what number this one was. Soon Owen wouldn't care about much, or at least that was the plan.

The whiskey in the glass had barely wetted his lips when Owen heard the doorbell. With a sigh, he put the drink down. It was a little early for Hilary to be showing up half drunk and begging to get back into his bed, but Owen guessed that it depended on how early she had started drinking. He definitely wasn't drunk enough to let her in. Owen went to the door anyway.

He didn't bother with the peephole because the person would be too fuzzy to see anyway. But it wasn't Hilary standing on his front step. It was Don and a supermodel dressed for partying.

"Hi," Don said, "Heard about your argument with Hilary and thought you could use some company to keep the demons at bay."

"Singular," Owen replied.

"This is my friend, Tiffany," Don said, "She is smarter than she looks."

"I could tell that by the fact that you called her a friend and not you girlfriend," Owen said, "Come in and welcome to the pity party." Owen held the door open and the two stepped inside. The door was closed and the three moved into the kitchen, where Owen took out two more glasses.

"So, you are not getting back together with this girl?" Tiffany asked. She had a slight accent and Owen realized it wasn't a tan but her actual skin tone.

"I've been stupid enough to do it before," Owen answered, "I don't plan to do it again."

"What are you going to do with this house then?" Don asked, "Since you claimed to have brought it for her."

"I'm selling it and the rings to a guy named Dave," Owen answered, "His girlfriend made the big announcement last week and he is panicking to get everything, except my clothing and toiletries, for a very cheap price and he is supposed to be over to sign the paperwork tomorrow along with bringing me the check. All I have to do is stay away from Hilary and her schemes until then."

"We can help with that," Tiffany smiled at Owen.

"Excellent," Owen smiled back before lifting his glass. Their glasses clinked before the booze was emptied from them.

Hilary pulled in behind the unfamiliar truck sitting in Owen's driveway. As she got out of her car, she studied the vehicle. The tailgate was down and there were several large boxes in the back. It was hard to tell whether the person was moving in or moving out. Confused Hilary went up the path to the house.

The front door was open, but the screen was closed. As Hilary opened the screen, which squeaked, a man stepped out of the living room. This man was completely unfamiliar to Hilary.

"Hello," the man said, "You must be Hilary."

"Where is Owen?" Hilary asked.

"He sold me the house two days ago," the man answered, "He said you would be around to collect your box of things." The man pointed to a box sitting beside the door.

"He sold the house?" Hilary asked, "Why would he sell the house, he loved this place?"

"I don't know," the man said, "But he was in a hurry to sell it; said something about needing a vacation."

"Did he leave a forwarding address?" Hilary asked.

"Nope," the man answered, "He said that all the bills had been paid up and anything else was trash. He didn't seem to think that anyone else needed to know where he was."

Hilary wanted to ask a dozen other questions, but she saw that this man didn't have the answers she wanted. He just bought a house and did not ask Owen about his plans from there. She looked down at the box and it did hold everything she had left at Owen's house over the time they dated.

"Did he say anything else?" Hilary asked hoping for something other than the dismissal she was receiving.

"Sorry, no," the man said.

"Okay," Hilary said as she bent down to pick up the box,

"Thank you." Hilary left the house with the box. She took it to her car and put it in the trunk before getting into the driver's seat. Hilary started the car and pulled out of the driveway.

She didn't get far down the road before she had to pull over and slam her hand down on the steering wheel in anger. How could he do that to her!

Owen could feel the dryness of his mouth along with the fuzziness of his tongue. His head suggested remaining in that position, but his bladder was ordering him to get up. Owen opened his eyes to find himself in a sun-lighted room and long silky, brown hair covering the pillow next to him. Looking around, the room didn't really seem familiar. There was a door was leading to a bathroom near a closed door leading somewhere else. The other two walls had large windows in them, which was where the sun was shining in through the curtains.

Owen slid out of bed and staggered to the bathroom, where he let the pressure on his bladder ease off. He glanced around the bathroom and noticed his toiletries as well as those of a female. However, Owen knew they couldn't be Hilary's because she had short, spikey hair. After flushing, Owen washed his hands and noticed he was wearing a wedding band on his left ring finger. It was new enough that it fit snuggly.

Once his hands were dry, Owen went back into the bedroom. He looked at the woman taking up one side of the bed. It was Don's friend, Tiffany. Her left hand was visible and she wore a matching wedding band along with an engagement ring.

Owen tried to remember what had happened after that first drink with Don and Tiffany, but nothing was coming to mind. If Tiffany was in his bed, Owen wondered where Don was. Curious about something else, Owen went to the window. He pushed aside the curtain and looked out. His vision was filled with palm trees, sandy beaches, and clear ocean.

There was the sound of someone moving around in bed.

"Everything all right?" Tiffany's voice made Owen feel weak in the knees, among other things.

"Everything is fine," Owen said as he turned back towards the bed and smiled at her, "Just fine."

THREE DAYS GONE

Hannah sat in the diner checking her phone for messages as she waited for her food. It had been three days since she had heard from her husband and she expected him to be panicking any day now. He was known to be a workaholic, but he should have noticed that she hadn't been there to cook meals or clean the house.

Hannah had come home with some good news and she couldn't wait to tell Desmond. But he hadn't been there. Having looked around, Hannah realized she had not seen him for forty-eight hours. It didn't look like he had been home as anything he might have touched was the same as when Hannah last cleaned.

Suddenly Hannah thought of all those times when he was gone for days at a time. The first time he used work as an excuse, but he hadn't bothered with any excuses since then. That was almost a year ago. His job had never gone beyond five before that and she was pretty sure it hadn't actually changed. There was also the lady who looked smugly at Hannah on the few times Hannah had gone to work functions with him since then. When Hannah suggested she could skip going to his work functions, he had been relieved but he tried not to let it show in front of her.

Since he had been gone for a few days for 'work', nothing was good enough for him. She didn't keep the house clean enough. Her cooking was subpar and she never made his favourites anymore. He blamed her job for taking up all of her time. The one she worked two days a week from nine to two, when he wasn't home to notice anyway. She never brought any work home.

The other change that had happened was her husband started sleeping in the guest room. When he started it was because he 'didn't want to disturb her' and thus thought it best when he came in late. Then a few months ago he had complained she didn't pay any attention to him. It matched the rest of the accusations he had thrown at her that day. She got mad enough to walk out of the house and crash at her sister's place. It had been a safe haven from him because he had never gotten along with her sister.

But he had won her back with false promises and a jewellery set she had wanted for months. The jewellery set Hannah had sold on her way out of town along with several of his other gifts from the past year. The ones he had brought home when she started questioning his working situation or appeared to be tempted to wander outside their sham of a marriage.

Because Hannah was sitting there remembering that she hadn't seen her husband in days and made a decision. She packed up what she wanted to keep and a bag of things worth selling into her car. The car she had bought with money from her job so he could not demand to have his name on the registration. Hannah had phoned the lawyer her husband had used for any legal questions and asked him to represent her if she needed it. He agreed after hearing the whole explanation from her. Then she had left the house that had become the cage for her marriage.

It was now the second morning after she had left. Her

husband had not sent any messages to tell her that he had missed her. She had called the lawyer before coming to this café for breakfast and he would start the paper work later today. He also figured it wouldn't take long for the whole process to go through, as long as her soon-to-ex-husband didn't dispute anything.

Hannah's food arrived. She ate while staring out the window. It was beautiful country out here. She had grown up in that town and had only ever been as far as her aunt's house, which was only a couple kilometres away. The drive has been quite nice and the autumn colours were starting to appear in the trees. Hannah wondered what the rest of the country looked like. She had money to find out until the divorce was settled and she was free of her husband.

When she was finished eating, Hannah paid the bill and left the café. She dropped the cellphone in the garbage can on her way to her car. Once at her car, Hannah smiled as she got inside at her thought. He would never know what her good news was.

THE BEST BROWNIE RECIPE

Makes 48 brownies

2 cups all-purpose flour
2 cups granulated sugar
1 cup butter or margarine
1 cup water
¼ cup dark, unsweetened cocoa
½ cup buttermilk
2 eggs
1 tsp. baking soda
1 tsp. vanilla
Frosting:
½ cup butter or margarine
2 Tbsp. dark cocoa
¼ cup milk
3 ½ cups unsifted powdered sugar
1 tsp. vanilla

In a large mixing bowl, combine the flour and sugar. In heavy saucepan, combine butter, water and cocoa. Stir and heat to boiling. Pour boiling mixture over the flour and sugar in bowl. Add the buttermilk, eggs, baking soda and vanilla. Mix well, using wooden spoon or high speed on electric mixer. Pour into a well buttered 17 ½ by 11-inch jellyroll pan. Bake at 400^0 F for twenty minutes or until brownies test done in centre. While brownies bake, prepare the frosting. In a saucepan, combine the butter, cocoa and milk. Heat to boiling, stirring. Mix in the powdered sugar and vanilla until frosting is smooth. Pour warm frosting over brownies as soon as you take them out of the oven. Cool.

The Best Brownie Recipe

B. Heather Mantler

ABOUT THE AUTHOR

Heather Mantler is a lover of fairy tales and fables. Her home town is Prince George, British Columbia. Heather is always working on another story as she hopes to finish every story idea that she has ever written down. She was a nominee for the fiction category of the 2012 Prince George Regional Arts and Cultural Awards and short listed for the 2013 John Harris Fiction Awards. Her blog is heathersdomain.wordpress.com. Heather encourages her readers to post reviews on Good Reads and Amazon.

www.ingramcontent.com/pod-product-compliance
Lightning Source LLC
Chambersburg PA
CBHW020741250626
47155CB00003B/866